BLACK WIDOW

BLACK WIDOW

By:

MICHELE WALLACE CAMPANELLI

ARPress LLC
45 Dan Road Suite 5
Canton MA 02021
Hotline: 1(888) 821-0229
Fax: 1(508) 545-7580

Ordering Information:
Quantity sales. Special discounts are available on quantity purchases by corporations, associations, and others. For details, contact the publisher at the address above.

Printed in the United States of America.

ISBN-13:   Softcover   979-8-89330-191-5
                 Hardcover   979-8-89330-193-9
                 eBook   979-8-89330-192-2

Library of Congress Control Number: 2024901773

DEDICATION

This book is dedicated to the members of my heavy metal rock band **Black Widow**: Dawn Kreiselman (Guitar), Kristen Pepper-Kirschten (Bass), and Dawn Serencko (Drums).

During the early 90s in the great state of Florida, I was nicknamed Screech and was Black Widow's lead singer. Those were the best and the wildest days of my youth. I can't thank the three of you enough. We were one of the first all-female rock bands in the United States of America. We broke the mold, all the rules and made history with songs about women's rights and helping the environment. We helped pave the way for femalerock musicians today. Thanks for all the great memories!

I'd also like to thank God, my wonderful husband Louis V. Campanelli III, my brother David & Greg, and the entire Wallace and Campanelli family.

A special thank you goes out to Fontaine Wallace, my personal editor and wonderful mother.

My deepest appreciation goes to Whiskey Creek Press especially Stephen Womack, Debra Womack, Melanie Billings, Gemini Judson, Sara Kent, and Marsha Briscoe for all the hard work that went into this novel's publication.

To God be the glory!

The Lord is near to the broken hearted,
and saves the crushed in spirit.
- Psalm 34:18

Contents

CHAPTER 1

And so, it began...

Chasing her through the alleys of New Orleans, I followed through the crowded streets running as fast as I could, pushing everyone out of my way. My gun out from its holster, I yelled, "Stop or I'll shoot!"

She ran into the back entrance of a hotel, the white diamond belt dangling around her small waist. When I got to the door, it was locked. Kicking it down was easy enough. Screams came from the hotel guests as I rushed into the lobby, my gun pointed out.

Many dropped to the floor, others ran toward the exits, but I wouldn't stop until I got her in my sight again. Through every hallway I checked and then I spied a black leather pant leg turning a corner.

Without a second to think about it, I flew after her and discovered that it wasn't a hall but a door on the other side. I rammed it down with my shoulder and entered a vacant hotel room only to find the woman about to jump out of the window.

"Stop, I mean it! Give me back those diamonds!"

She turned. This time I saw her face. Encircled by long, raven black hair, her features were small and sweet. If I caught her on the street walking past, I'd think she looked more like a good girl than what she really was: very, very bad.

Her brilliant silver-blue eyes flashed as she stepped down and held up her hands. "You've proven yourself a proper adversary," she said.

"Adversary?" I wondered what she meant. "Just keep them up, Lady."

"Let me introduce myself," she said. "My name is Blackie, and I am the Widow."

Slowly, she came forward and I couldn't help noticing her large breasts stuffed into that leather cat suit. She had a figure, all right, and those eyes. She lined them like Cleopatra. I had to admit to myself, if we hadn't met this way, I'd beg for a date since she was quite beautiful.

"I love diamonds," she said. "Big ones, small ones, they are all in my collection. Do you like chasing me, Museum Guard? Did you really think you were going to stop me from taking this belt prize?" Her hand rubbed over the giant gems around her middle.

"Take it off," I roared. "My boss would have my head if I let you get away with that ancient Egyptian piece."

"How about we forget you catching me at all?" Blackie stepped over to me, pushing the gun slowly down.

"Have you no fear?" I asked her.

"I have no shame." She kissed my lips suddenly.

For some reason, I decided not to push her off. She wrapped her hands around my back, and I couldn't stop myself from wanting those lips. She shoved me onto the bed and started removing my shirt. Over and over, she kissed my chest and I felt suddenly helpless. She pulled a pair of handcuffs out from a leather boot and cuffed one hand to the bedpost.

In a trance, I couldn't do anything to resist. This woman wanted me too and I didn't care about anything else. She could take my gun, shoot me and I knew at any moment, she just might.

Then slowly, she took the gun out of my hand. "You're making this too easy for me," she said.

"Is that what you are, easy?"

"A little," she admitted as she lowered her frame and began kissing my left nipple.

I felt her nails dig into my sides and on my back and enjoyed every second of it until it came, the bite. It wasn't painful. In fact, it had pleasure mixed in. I glanced down to my shoulder and watched her pull her teeth from my flesh. No blood came.

"Will I need a rabies shot?" I asked. Then she rose off of me and smiled.

I could hear the sirens coming and knew she was about to be on her way. It had nothing to do with me. In fact, for a brief moment, sadness crept across my face. "Leaving, already?" I asked.

"Things to do," she said.

"Will I see you again?"

"Oh, you've been bitten. I think so."

"What do you mean?" I asked her.

Cops burst into the room; gun fire began. She cocked my gun and started shooting them back out of the room. One cop got hit in the leg and dropped to the floor. He scooted back. Then his hands went up, but she didn't shoot him again. This gave her just enough time to jump for the window. As she did, the latch caught the sleeve of her leather cat suit, ripping it slightly. Beneath was a tattoo of a black spider with a red hourglass in the middle.

Another officer went in pursuit to the window and looked down. He turned his head and spoke into the box next to his neck. "She's driving a black sports car...maybe a corvette of some type? Can't see the license, wait a minute. It's under the light. It reads D- I- E- M- E- N-S."

Suddenly a smile crossed my lips. I suddenly realized what name she had given me. Blackie Widow. This woman named herself after one of the most deadly spiders in the world, the black widow.

The cop stood over me, without my shirt on, and hand cuffed. "She didn't bite you, did she?" he asked.

"Why?" I wondered.

"Where?" He frantically began searching my body.

"My shoulder," I told him.

He checked the red mark and sighed. "Good, she didn't break the skin that much."

"She scratched me," I admitted.

"That's okay, as long as she didn't bite you hard."

"What? Is she deadly?" I questioned, almost laughing.

The cop ran his hand over the wound. "The FBI's been tracking her for over three years. She's stolen over four million dollars worth of diamonds worldwide, hurt twenty-six men with a stun gun. There's a rumor associated with her with those who get too close. Trust me, you don't want to know."

"What?" I wanted to. "Tell me."

"She's just like the spider. Every man who's ever been bitten dies in some kind of accident later."

"Rumors," I said and laughed.

He shot at the hand cuffs, and I was set free. A sick feeling came over me as I sat up.

"Was he bit?" Another officer who rushed into the room asked me.

"No," I said.

"Good," he replied, then bent down to assist the cop holding his thigh from a bullet graze wound and bleeding over the Persian carpet.

"You can't be serious about this?" I asked. "She's just a woman. The only real damage is a broken heart, right?"

The cop smiled, but somehow that didn't reassure me.

CHAPTER 2

"Good morning," a voice said.

I knew before even looking up from the security guard's desk that he was a player. His pants were two sizes too big, and his underwear was slightly showing at the rim. The voice even had a sarcastic tone. "Who are you?"

"A private investigator who heard you had a little visit from my girl last night."

This got my attention, so I glanced at his face. Short and thick, he was bald and was wearing shades even though it was night. His features were perfect. In fact, he appeared more like a man out of a fashion magazine.

"By the look of your wrist she must have had you tied up," he said and smiled. "You are the museum security guard that let her get away last night, right?"

Around his neck was a large silver chain that half blinded me. "What do you want?"

"Let's just say information."

"If you don't mind, I have a ton of paperwork. I almost lost my job thanks to the robbery last night."

"I hear you," he mumbled. "My name's Martin. I won't take up much of your time. Just want you to answer a couple of questions, that's all."

I stopped writing and put down the pen. Never met a private investigator before, even considered the profession after graduating from college. I thought that was another choice until I saw the advertisement for a museum guard. "So, who hired you to ask me questions?"

"Me. That diamond ring she wears around her fourth finger is worth two hundred fifty thousand dollars. Since your museum robbery, the reward went up to two million for the diamonds to be returned to their proper owners. There is also a bounty for her for far less, but I'm not interested in her, just the diamonds."

"I didn't see a giant ring on her finger." I remembered her hands, fondly. They were small, but perfectly shaped. The nails were short but painted blood red.

"No, ring, huh? She don't wear it all the time, I guess. Rumor has it she puts it on right before going to bed naked." A grin curved across his lips.

He's seen her. I knew by the smile; it made a pit form in my stomach. "She has quite a circle of rumors around her."

"You've been bitten." Martin turned to walk away. "Looks like you won't be much help to me after all."

I stopped him. "She stole an ancient Egyptian diamond and river stone belt worth almost a million from the storage room of our museum last night. If you find her, I want it back. Her stealing happened on my watch. My boss has been on the phone all morning with the cops."

"Did she break the skin?" he wanted to know.

I pulled down my collar and showed him. Now it was a large red mark; a slight scratch was at the top.

Martin glanced away. "Could be worse."

"What do you mean?"

"You like this job?" he asked.

"It's a living." I hated being alone in this stuffy place. Sitting in a museum all night with nothing to do but stare at dead people painted on the walls and ancient items got old quick. At least working retail store security there were customers to talk to.

"Well, turns out I'm looking for a new partner. That's how she got away last night. She might have some friends now and I could use the extra fire power. You know how to use that piece of junk?"

He pointed to my gun which never had actually been used, only pointed. "Yes."

"We get back the diamonds. We split the reward money. Several million dollars for even part of the jewelry she's stolen."

"Sounds like a dangerous bounty," I said.

"It isn't a job for pussy-whipped white folk, but since she scared off one of my brothers and I can't find a permanent replacement, guess you'll do, since you know about her."

"You'll pay me a salary?"

"I hear ya. I'll pay double what you're making now working at this joint."

I looked down at the pile of papers on my desk; the thought of another night trapped in this place, bored, didn't appeal to me. No, this job was okay if you had a wife and kid to make your life interesting at home, but I didn't. This was all I had, and that didn't add up to a hill of beans. Slowly, not knowing if I was making the biggest mistake of my life, I raised my hand. "We've got a deal, Martin. I'll help you return the stolen diamonds by tracking the Widow."

He shook my hand. "I've only got five rules for working with me. One, I drive the car. Two, don't touch my ride. Three, you can have sex with as many big-ass women as possible but not mine. Four, shoot everyone who has a gun pointed at you. And the most important rule, stay the hell out of my way. Got it?"

"I hear you." I rose from my desk.

"You got anything to wear other than that, white boy?"

"Don't call me boy. And I'm actually Italian. For the record this Italian likes big-ass women too."

He chuckled. "Looks like we'll get along fine then. I was right, after all.

I knew you'd take this job."

I walked around the desk, shrugging. "Why were you so sure?"

"You got that bitten fire in your eyes."

"My name's Romeo Maroni," I told him. "My friends call me Rome."

"Don't kid yourself, Romeo. I've seen it before. Once bitten, and they all get that way. Some fade away completely from the thirst of her, but you, you're going to last until you catch what bit you."

"What are you talking about?" I wondered, grabbing my flashlight and gym bag.

"Obsession, it's a dangerous thing when it comes to Blackie Widow. Believe me, I know. I've never been bitten, but I've heard. The bite grows on you until you don't know if you hate or love her. She's evil and like an angel all wrapped up into one. She gets under your skin and no matter how many times you try to kill the memory, she just keeps coming back. One thing is for sure when you're dealing with a dangerous woman, you can't forget her no matter how hard you try. Some men relish the thought of even having her again, but others, well, just the thought makes them go mad."

"Save the romantic advice for someone looking."

"A single man's always looking." Martin laughed. "You're just lookin' in the wrong neighborhood. You should try what the brothers like to flavor. Maybe I can cure you of her venom."

"You really think I'll become obsessed with the Black Widow? Come on, she's beautiful, but not my type."

"Who likes a nice girl? What man wants his momma in his bed?"

"Good point." I laughed.

"Trust me, that girl is pleasure, but can any man survive after the load comes out, if you know what I'm saying."

"I took this job to get back diamonds, Martin. The money, not the girl, believe me. She doesn't interest me at all." Even as I said it, I knew it was a lie. From the way he smiled back, I could tell he didn't believe me either.

CHAPTER 3

The second my feet hit the pavement, I spotted the unusual car parked right in front. The vehicle was long like a Caprice with no top. The dark blue paint had specks of silver which sparkled in the sunlight. Flame décor shot from one chrome bumper to the other. With a few more steps, I inspected the interior. It was a lighter shade of blue and silver. The steering wheel looked like a giant round chain and an air freshener hung from the stereo system which had more buttons than an airplane. Instead of pine shaped, the freshener was an outlined naked woman.

"Let me guess, your ride."

"It's dope. I know." Martin jumped in without opening the door.

I lowered my hand to the chain door handle and quickly sat down on the flamed seat cushions. "I'm not sure if I should be seen in this thing."

"Don't worry. No one ever notices my car," Martin said, sarcastically.

With a flip of the key, the engine roared ten times louder than any other car on the road. Suddenly the back flew up and then the front.

"Hydraulics, you cannot be serious? Shouldn't we blend? I mean we are private investigators."

"It's reverse shrink-ism. You see. The more we stand out the less likely they'll think we're tracking anyone." Martin grinned. "This is my dream ride."

"My nightmare." I held on to the side of the car for dear life.

Martin laughed for a moment and then pushed a button that made the vehicle level out. He drove from the parking lot and continued down the main road. After a few streets, his head turned at a woman walking down the street. "Hey, baby," he said and waved. The woman gave him a nasty look.

"You sure are a ladies' man," I said, trying not to chuckle.

"She just wasn't in the mood. I had her twelve times last week. Now let's forget about the finer sex and get down to business." Martin leaned over. "Off my police scanner last night, the cops tracked a black Corvette going into this garage. Blackie parked and took another car out. That's when the cops lost her."

"They get prints off the car?"

"Nope," he said. "They never do."

He drove his hot rod into a three-story parking garage. It was full of vehicles of all types, a few trucks, mostly SUVs. On the second level, Martin pulled over and parked in the only empty spot.

"This is it, the spot. CSI taped this and took pictures."

Sweat dripped off my forehead, so I slowly wiped it off. As I was getting out of the car my head started to spin a little. I grabbed the door. For a second I had to lean against the largest part of the flames.

"You okay, bro?"

"Yeah," I said.

"Sure? You're looking kind of pale."

"I just didn't eat anything since last night," I explained.

"Diabetic?"

I nodded. "My blood sugar's low."

"I've got some potato chips in the glove box."

Wondering how long they'd been in there; I shoved my hand into the compartment in front of the passenger's seat. Sure enough, a bag of chips sat unopened. I immediately opened the bag and began to munch away. Although I began to feel stronger almost right away, something was wrong. My head was throbbing, and my knees started to tremble slightly.

Martin didn't pay me much attention. He was scanning our surroundings. Next to us was a garbage can which obviously had been looked at by police. It was completely empty even with all this walking traffic.

"Nothing," Martin said.

"What did you expect?" I asked. "It's not like..." Then a drainage grate below my foot caught my eye. Trapped inside, just a corner of a notebook. "She left a notebook."

"What?" Martin stepped over and peered in. The second he saw it, he pulled off the grate and looked at the book. It was leather and completely dry because of the weeks of lack of rain. His fingers ran over the outside. "Beautiful," he said. "The Black Widow diary."

He was right. The outside was in perfect condition. Black as night, the pages opened up. Whoever wrote upon these pages, wrote in sharp red pen. On the first page was a full-scale map of the inside of the museum. What followed were notes of where all the cameras were placed. "*One right, twodoors down. Four on the second level, avoid first floor stairs*" it read.

"Bingo," Martin said.

Suddenly I felt faint and leaned back onto the car.

"You're not looking so good." Martin closed the book.

"I'm okay." I pulled out my blood tester. The small blue prick needle rose to my finger. It hurt only for a second. After I placed a small drop of blood on the strip, it instantly revealed my sugar levels. It read 115.

Martin said, "My momma had that sugar disease until she grew twelve humps on her back."

"I'm fine. Thanks for letting me know that."

"I'm joshing." Martin's eyes twinkled. "Well, if it ain't your blood, what the hell's the matter with you?"

"Not funny." A pain hit me sharp in my lower region, a soreness I hadn't noticed before. "Ouch."

"What?"

"Take me to the hospital," I said, getting back into the car. "Take me there now! It could be my appendix."

Martin tossed the book into the back seat, jumped into the driver's side and sped out of the garage. I was trying not to think of the unusual feeling I had in my lower right side and my male area. A place I didn't want to be ill. Ever.

I noticed how well Martin drove. He was speeding past car after car, cutting trucks off left and right. Normally, I'd be scared of any driver so reckless, but this time I was very glad to have him behind the wheel. Martin must have been in many car chases as a private investigator/bounty hunter, I decided. Ones he didn't ever lose.

As the car pulled into the hospital's emergency lane, my eyes were drawn to a nurse. Her hair was tied into a bun. It was odd. The bun was not on the back of her head, but like a ball on the very top. I found it intriguing why she wore her hair like an Oriental. Was she, I wondered? Then my attention went to the features on her petite little face.

Beautiful.

She wore red lipstick the color of a rose, her eyes lined like Cleopatra. Those crystal silver-blue eyes shot back at me. I'd never forget that face as long as I lived. This woman before me was the Black Widow all men feared.

"Martin," I called, but he was running away for a nurse to get me help.

I couldn't move well. My whole body felt sore, like I'd run a marathon and for some reason every cut that she had sliced into my back yesterday with her red nails hurt so much worse at this very moment.

The disguised nurse leaned over me and said, "Welcome to my web." Feeling the intense pain in my lower male region, I reached out to her, but my hand came hurdling back as I slowly passed out.

CHAPTER 4

In a panic, my eyes flashed opened. Inside a small hospital room, I discovered that I lay in a bed covered in white sheets. Sitting next to me was Martin, holding Blackie's diary closed on his lap. Above him was a brilliant white light and behind him a window had shades drawn shut.

"Where is that nurse?" I asked.

His round, tough face suddenly smiled. "Finally woke up and had to ask about the ladies, huh?"

"Where is the nurse, the Black Widow?"

He chuckled. "You're even dreaming about Blackie already. She got you bad, boy. Didn't your momma ever tell you to turn away from the wild ones? I learned that in Bible class when I was five."

Sitting up, I noticed that I had an IV needle taped to my arm. A line ran up to a bag sitting on a metal holder. For a second I wondered what drugs they were putting in me, but a sudden pain made me not care. "Ouch!" My hands flew to my male anatomy, and I groaned in agony. In all my years with only one urinary tract infection and a pool stick hitting accidentally there, I realized neither had hurt this bad.

"Take it easy, you don't want the ladies knowing you got some problems."

"What the hell is the matter with my dick?"

Martin said pensively, "They don't know. I told the doctors you were grabbing so they put a line in to test your pee. You're fine; except you're all red. I even told them about your sugar, and they said your numbers were good. They think it might be some virus so they are giving you penicillin through the IV which should cure the dick infection.”

Slowly I lifted the sheet and raised the gown carefully. Sure enough my best friend was pink and raw. I didn’t dare touch it because I knew it would hurt. “What is this? I mean it feels like I got laid twenty times or something.”

Treating me evasively, Martin didn’t respond until finally he said, “You don’t want to know what I think.”

I lowered the blanket. It felt as if I had run a marathon. My back hurt too. Those scratches felt as if she had just sliced my skin. When I closed my eyes, I could still hear her breath against my ear. “But she was here. I saw her.”

“You’ve been napping for hours.”

“She came. I saw Blackie.”

Tossing the book onto my chest, Martin rose. “This game isn’t for boys with white-size dicks. Stop lying.”

My fear changed to anger. “I’m your partner now. I want to know what is going on so if you know something, you better tell me! Did you see her? Where did she go?”

“The truth is difficult for even a brother to understand,” Martin said.

I reached up and grabbed his arm. Around his wrist was a large silver bracelet that twisted into two braids. It made a clicking noise as his hand shook but Martin paid it no mind. Instead, he sat down and took a deep breath, pondering over if he should tell me what he knew. “Come on, let’s have it.”

“All right,” he said. “This happened once before to a cop about three years ago. He claimed he never was bitten either, but he ended up in the hospital complaining of the same thing, redness of the Johnson and scratches on the back. He said something about how it felt like it was on fire. Then he went half-crazy over her, said he couldn’t stop wanting her.”

“She scratched my back too,” I said.

"I thought that brother was off his rocker. But maybe since you are going through the same thing there's something more."

"You think she drugged me through her nails?"

"They tested for drugs. No, you weren't given anything," Martin said. "She's the bad thing."

He flipped open the book and turned to the third page. Raising it slightly so I could read, he pointed to a line. It read only, *"DIEMENS" aren't a girl's best friend."*

"She does kind of look like a brunette Marilyn. She just has longer hair and is a bit more on the dangerous side. Don't think I'd want to see Blackie again if I were you. If you change your mind about being my sidekick, I'll understand."

My eyes focused on the words; just below the hateful phrase, scratched were, *"KD100 security door to the left, bring a card."* I remembered what my boss had said about the only diamond bigger than what was on that belt was the Ken Delsey one hundred carat diamond bracelet. "Do you know about the Ken Delsey diamond bracelet?"

Martin glanced down to the note. "You could be right. This could be a clue to what her next target might be. I'll make a few calls and look into that diamond bracelet. You rest." He headed for the door in a hurry.

"Marty," I called. "I'm still your partner, right?"

He nodded, but I saw a hint of disappointment. He no longer truly trusted my judgment and quite frankly neither did I. Not totally wrong, the girl had gotten under my skin, literally. I didn't know why, but just holding this book made me feel better. Even though every fiber in my body feared her, I wanted her kiss again. I remembered how she felt in my arms, how sweet she seemed yet so wrong.

I wasn't about to believe all these rumors Martin was spinning. She was just a woman, not a monster, a girl with a taste for expensive things. Perhaps she was the product of abuse. That's why she'd come to despise men and only take what they offered. Whatever issues she had in the past, Blackie was a woman who could be cured, I believed. A woman with so much beauty and intelligence, she had to offer the world more than just insanity and fear.

I flipped the page and saw what was written. *"Romeo, Security Guard,is a distraction."* That was written in red. Chills ran up my spine to know that is what she thought of me, merely as a distraction. Wasn't I her wonderful knight in shining armor? Was I just a target? Clearly, this was more than just notes on paper, this was like a diary of her criminal deeds even before they happened, and she'd even written my name.

Underneath her words, Martin had scribbled beneath in blue ink. The writing was larger, and the words immediately made me know he wrote it. *"Rome was her marked man."*

When he came back in the room, his face loomed. I knew something was wrong and I guessed we were already late with the KD100. Martin sat back down and folded his legs. "She shot another cop four times with a stun gun to get away. She went too far; he might have permanent damage to his leg. The cops are out for blood now, Rome."

"Then she got away again." I said, almost happily.

Martin turned to the next page of Blackie's diary and pointed to the drawing. There was simply a giant diamond spider drawn on a necklace with the words "My kind don't like water." He nodded and said, "If we can't find her soon, hope you like cruises."

CHAPTER 5

After being released, Martin drove up to a small white house not far from the hospital. In the front were several yellow and pink hibiscus trees and hanging ferns. It didn't seem like a house Martin would live in. No, this was too normal. In front of the windows were tiny flower boxes with bright red Zinnias.

"You coming?" he asked.

I studied him for a moment as he put on his shades and straightened his shirt. Then I knew immediately, this must be a lady's house and not his at all. He pulled up his pants and tightened the belt, checked himself in the mirror and glanced over. "Don't take all day."

I got slowly out of the flame-painted vehicle and followed him up the driveway. By the garage was a porch swing, a lawn mower and a few knickknacks and garden gnomes. Martin knocked on the door, and when he opened it, I saw his expression change from one of nervousness to complete happiness.

This must be his girlfriend.

She stood a good six foot five, with flaming red hair even though her dark skin was the same tone as his. Her body wasn't lean; in fact, most men would say she was morbidly obese. Her butt was quite huge but there was something charming about her face. She had the smile of an angel and eyes that seemed to light up the second she saw him. Martin leaned over and kissed her quickly on the lips.

"Hey, baby, this is my boy, Romeo," Martin introduced. "He's my new partner. And, Rome, this is my leading lady, Tye."

"Romeo, Romeo, where for art the white men in this neighborhood," she said and giggled, sweetly. "Come on in. I just made some fresh meatballs and garlic toast on linguini noodles."

"That's right up Rome's alley," Martin said, glancing over at me.

"I really should get back to my place and rest," I said, suddenly feeling like I was intruding on a couple destined to be. "It's only about a mile. I can walk."

"No way, Rome." Tye grabbed my arm. "Now you come right in and sit a spell. Don't you know it's insultin' not to eat my balls?"

Trying to stop my mind from going in the gutter, I smiled. My stomach was a bit hungry after all and I had already gotten an insulin shot at the hospital. Perhaps it wouldn't be bad to taste her cooking. I had to admit to myself, this girl was a sweetheart. Within two minutes I liked her more than Martin.

Walking further in, I took a quick look around the room. It was very nicely decorated with matching colors, pictures of unfamiliar faces in the hallway; all accept one of Martin and her at the beach. She was heavy in a one piece but there was no denying how happy they appeared with arms around each other. Still feeling achy in my region, I sat down gently on the velvet, dark green sofa. Across from it was a matching chair with big satin pillows. Oh, this was nice, I thought, as my lower half sank down in the soft cushions.

"So, what kind of trouble are you two boys up to?" she asked as she set the table with white China plates. "I heard you got a bright red dick problem."

Leaning over, I couldn't help noticing the size of her breasts. Martin must have noticed me watching because he stood in my view, gazing down at me with angry eyes. "What was rule number three?"

I smiled, remembering how I was not to take his woman. Of course, I really didn't want her. It's just no man could not notice those enormous breasts. They were probably even real. "Ouch!" I screamed, grabbing myself.

"You okay?" Tye asked.

"He's still got problems down there," Martin said. "He's got white man's penis disease and it's making him sick to be in the presence of a much larger specimen."

Tye began placing linguini and meatballs with sauce on the plates. She winked at Martin and said, "Oh, is that right?" Her playful tone implied she didn't think he was that big.

When the plates were all full with food that smelled better than my own mother's, Martin sat down and I knew my parts would rise and go sit down too. Making my way, I walked as gently as I could. Tye sat down next to me while Martin began eating quickly.

"What about grace, Marty?" Tye asked.

"Oh, sorry, baby." He stopped and folded his hands.

Following his lead, I did the same while Tye blessed our dinner. We didn't speak much while we ate. It wasn't that I didn't enjoy their company. Tye's cooking was really great. I could have eaten another meatball even after another piece of garlic toast.

"I don't have dessert. Why don't we go down to the ice cream shop and pick up something for all of us?" Tye suddenly rose and began taking the empty plates back to the kitchen.

Martin nodded, checked his wallet and said, "You can get whatever you want tonight, baby."

"Oooooh, what about a brownie sundae in vanilla?"

"You got it, girl." Marty smiled.

"What about you, Rome?" Tye invited. "Would you like to come with us? They have twenty flavors of ice cream."

Feeling like a third wheel and just wanting to sit back on that very soft sofa, I said, "Just bring me back whatever, sugar-free."

Tye left the dishes in the sink. Martin rose from the table, and it didn't take him long to wrap his arm around her back and lead her to the door. He whispered in her ear, and she had a light laugh as they left.

Alone in Tye's crib, I moved back to the sofa and noticed that Martin had left Blackie's diary on the coffee table among Hollywood

Star magazines. I picked it up, sat back down, and a smile crossed my face. This was a very comfortable piece of furniture. Wish I could take a nap, I thought, with my eyes instantly feeling heavy.

The door behind me opened again and quickly shut.

"You want some money for the sugar-free?" I asked, glancing back to who I thought would be Martin.

There she was in a low-cut white sundress, plain with web straps across the bosom. Her raven hair falling down her pale white shoulders only made her red rose lips stand out even more. She took my breath away.

"You have something of mine," she said, raising her hand as if I would hand it to her.

"The Black Widow," I said, more surprised than a greeting.

She took a few steps closer, sat down next to me and grabbed the notebook. Why I didn't fight her, I didn't know. That was our one way of tracking her, but there was no need to follow her when she was right there in front of me. Her light eyes sparkled. My goodness, she was beautiful.

Instead of leaving, she smiled and I couldn't help but return the gesture. "How are you feeling?" she asked, knowingly.

"Pretty bad. What did you do to me?"

"Don't you like my venom?" she asked. "Love and hate me forever now?"

My brain told me to say no, but I nodded yes.

Suddenly her lips came at me so quickly I couldn't stop them. Her mouth took mine and I couldn't push her away. She broke the kiss as fast as it came, and it was a good thing because my lower half felt on fire now.

She stood and began heading for the door. How could she do that? Kiss me, take her notebook back and want to go so easily. She was a thief, a dangerous broad and I'm acting like a school boy with a crush. Finding the courage, I rose and went after her.

An elbow came at my chest and I felt the blow. It didn't knock me over, but I lost the air in my lungs. My hand went into a fist, but I couldn't strike. I grabbed her arm instead and she gave me a kick that landed me on the floor.

She tilted her head and chuckled. "Do you really think you can stop me?" She stressed the word "you" as if I were no threat at all.

"Give the book back," I ordered.

"It's mine," she stated as she opened the door and walked out.

I should have gone after her, but I didn't. Too busy watching her walk away, I was enjoying the view of her legs and feeling the rush of wanting them wrapped around me. Whatever venom this lady put through my veins was now messing with my head too. My brain throbbed and I realized Martin was right. I wasn't going to be much help to him after all.

CHAPTER 6

Women and spiders! Who knew? Shouldn't they all like something cuter like butterflies or kittens? Spiders are rumored to give a home good luck. I never understood that old wives tale. Maybe it has something to do with killing bugs. I'd rather squash them than leave them to build more nests.

What a fool I am!

Thinking it over and over, I couldn't help but feel horrible that I practically handed away evidence that could have helped Martin. In retrospect, I should have throttled her. Tossed that tight body to the ground and kept her hostage until the police arrived.

Most men would have. But not me; no, I'm the idiot that let her go. Of course, we know what her next target already is because of that diary. It's on a cruise ship. Blackie's going after the spider necklace worn by one of the wealthiest women that live in our city: the wife of a major league player. He's known as Mr. Baseball and he's one of the richest men in America, making over twenty million dollars a season. His wife is a forensic bug scientist who has a thing about spiders too.

Women and spiders! Who knew? Shouldn't they all like something cuter like butterflies or kittens? Spiders are rumored to give a home good luck. I never understood that old wives tale. Maybe it has something to do with killing bugs. I'd rather squash them than leave them to build more nests.

It didn't take long for Martin and Tye to return. Martin grabbed my shoulder and said, "Let's go! I saw Blackie get into another black Corvette around the corner!" He then kissed Tye. "Sorry, baby, work's callin'."

Not wanting to tell him right away about my losing Blackie's diary, I thanked Tye as I ran and followed Martin back to the unusual car. I sat down carefully but in a hurry and held on as he sped off.

"Oh here." He tossed me a bag.

Inside was a cup of ice cream. I knew I couldn't eat it now, but man did I want to. Ahead, in traffic, was a long black 'Vette. This one was older with the longer curvy front and had an unusual tail in the back.

"That's the car," Martin said, grabbing the ice cream cup. He started eating it right in front of me. With one arm, he drove with perfect precision, weaving in and out of traffic, eating while he ate what should have been my ice cream. "This is good, should have gotten another scoop of this for myself," he said.

"Wasn't that mine?" I asked.

"I didn't see any cash leaving your hands."

"How much you want for it?" I asked.

"It's almost all gone now." He tossed over the cup, and I peered in. He was right, only about a cup left. "Not bad for sugar-free."

Our car pulled up next to the sports car at a red light and I saw her again. She quickly gave us an unworried glance and then turned her gaze back to the light. On the dash was her black book. Martin must have seen it too because he gave me a quick smack on the shoulder.

"You gave her the diary back?"

"She took it," I said.

"And when were you going to tell me that she came to my crib?"

"Right after I ate my ice cream," I admitted.

Blackie Widow flipped us off and then moved the same insulting finger to point ahead. She revved her engine, making it clear she wanted to race.

"You've got to be kidding," I said.

Martin grinned and I knew immediately I better put my seat belt on and get it fastened. My hand rushed for the belt but there wasn't enough time. Tires screeched. My head flew back as both cars sped off.

The road ahead was filled with traffic, but neither driver wavered. Each car took a side on the three-lane highway and weaved in and out between the cars. Suddenly my body was thrown forward and hit the dash. Both cars stopped at another light. Her black vehicle sat one car in front of ours.

"She won this round," he said. "Don't worry, I'll take her on the highway."

Worried, I then snapped my seat belt lock, thanking God that I had time enough to do it at this light. Again, the tires screeched. Almost hitting the SUV in front of us, we sped around and Martin floored it. With no cars in front of him, he swerved to push her car onto the turn pike. Together we raced side by side at speeds near eighty miles an hour. It seemed faster but it didn't need to be.

Blackie's 'Vette hit the highway first and there she drove even faster, trying to leave us in the dust. Moving around a semi-truck, I almost lost the meatballs in my stomach. Martin wasn't about to give up. We rushed past the big rig and met her on the other side. Looking ahead, I could see both lanes were blocked by RVs.

"Take the wheel," Martin said.

"What?"

"Take it!" He jumped in the back seat.

Immediately I switched sides to drive. Martin was insane. What the hell was he doing? He stood in the back seat about to leap onto her car.

"Hold it steady!" he said.

"No way," I said and gasped.

Just as the last word left my mouth, Martin was in the air. He jumped and landed right on the large hood grabbing at the windshield to hold on. Blackie seemed surprised but not for long, she began to weave, trying to knock him off.

Martin was hanging on for dear life. He pulled himself up and curled himself over the windshield and sat down next to her. Grabbing for the book, Blackie smacked back Martin's hand. He raised a fist to punch her, and I rammed the 'Vette quickly.

He gave me a look of pure rage. "Don't you hurt my car!"

I nodded and he lowered his fist. Slowly, he grabbed the wheel from her and moved his foot to slow the car down on the shoulder. Slowly, both cars came to a stop. I parked behind hers.

Martin had a hand around her arm, yanking on her to get out of the car. "Just the diamonds!" he roared. "Give me what I want, and I'll give you ten minutes before I report seeing you to the cops, Miss Widow."

I got out of the car in a rush to protect her. Martin grimaced. "You can't be serious!"

He rose onto his feet, holding the notebook which she was desperately trying to snag back. She squirmed in his grasp, trying to push Martin away. He wasn't budging and underneath his tightening fingers, red marks began to appear. "Come on, don't grab her so hard. She'll tell us where the diamonds are. Won't you?"

Suddenly she stopped trying to get away from Martin. Her eyes turned to me and she smiled.

"Now that you two have had your little reunion, why don't you tell us where the diamonds are, Blackie, especially the ring and the museum belt?"

Then I saw it happen. She bit his arm so fast, I couldn't believe it. He screamed in horror, falling back over the door and out of the car. Her foot hit the gas pedal and the 'Vette took off at speeds unimaginable.

I ran for the flame-painted car to pursue, but Martin didn't move off the pavement. There was horror washing over his face. Then he began ripping at the wound and sucking as if to catch the poison. He spat out his own blood over and over.

Instead of chasing, I watched. Martin actually believed she had a poisonous bite? Again and again, he spat out the blood from his small wound. Then he ran to the ice cream cup, gulped what was left and spit it out. Coughing a few times, he then started whining. "Please, God, I don't want to die! Please! I'll marry Tye, my big-bootie woman. I'll make an honest woman out of her. Please, don't let me die!"

"You okay, Martin?" I asked him.

"How do I look?" he asked, grabbing at his eyes. "Are they blood shot? Do I look pale to you?"

I glanced over his black face and dark, clear eyes. "No."

"That's because she isn't nothing," he said, then handed me the notebook. "That's how a brother gets the book back. It takes a fine black man to get the job done."

I folded the diary in my arms. It felt good to have it back. We needed it to find the diamonds, I guessed. Perhaps locked in these pages were locations of where she stashed them.

Was Martin pretending to suck out the venom a joke or was he not faking? I wondered. Perhaps that display was to stop me from getting behind the wheel of his car.

Martin looked over his vehicle and noticed the dent on his car, and the scratch. "Rule number two is, never mess with my ride." He hopped back in the driver's side and motioned me to sit down.

The door wouldn't open so I pulled a Marty and hopped in. A smile crossed my face. "You were joking back there, right?" I asked, half hoping he didn't believe she was deadly as the rumors claimed. "You didn't really think her bite was deadly, right?"

Martin took a deep breath. Worry suddenly crossed his face as he rechecked the wound. It was still seeping blood. He had ripped at it enough to make it bleed for a while. His face suddenly turned to hide the panic. I knew he was still afraid.

CHAPTER 7

artin dropped me off at my apartment complex. Slumping from the pain of my injury and being bounced around in the car, I couldn't wait to crawl up those stairs and climb into my own bed. My place wasn't much, a one-bedroom studio apartment, but the second I tossed my key into the door I relaxed. Only a few steps and I'd get underneath the covers of my unmade sheets. Passing the kitchen filled with dirty plates and unwashed glasses, I moved past the paper bags of fast-food restaurants. The end of the room never looked so inviting. Not a piece of fancy artwork in the joint, not a knick knack or even one plant, just me and my bed. The only thing hanging on the walls was one giant Cubs poster. I was home.

I reached my bedroom and pulled down the covers on the mattress. I sighed as I climbed in. My eyes fluttered for a few minutes as I stared up at the moving fan which I must have left on. Around and around, it went, making swooshing noises.

As I rolled over, I saw a giant hole in my floor right next to my bed. I slipped off my bed and went to it. Breaking through several cobwebs, I leaned into the hole only to discover that the apartment below me was no longer occupied by an old couple. Now the place looked eerie, dark and full of webs. Jumping down into the web, I landed in the sticky substance. The string clung to me, but I didn't mind; my body slowly lowered to stand at the bottom.

Blackie Widow laid on top of a flat table, her back to me. Her bare bottom and long legs invited me to come closer for a better view of what appeared to be her very attractive naked body.

Music was playing, something I hadn't heard before. It was alluring, heavy and driving me forward. The drums mimicked my steps as I neared her. It was almost frightening, but not enough to stop me.

Her body was indeed naked as I had first thought, but not completely. As I drew closer, I saw them; hundreds of diamonds shimmered on the table under the one pale light in the room. Instead of her hair long and hanging, it was tied into a bun at the very back of her head. A string of diamonds tied the hairdo and just below a necklace hung the wrong way. It had a long strip of diamonds that fell from the nape of her neck to the top of her full bottom. My goodness-what a beauty! This had to be a dream. No woman could look this delicious. Her body began to move ever so slowly to the thump of the drums. Then she sat up onto her knees, still facing the wrong way. Her hands rolled through the diamonds and tossed them into the air. They rolled down her frame, hitting and falling off her luscious body onto the ground. One giant stone came to my feet. I didn't care to pick it up. It wasn't stones I was interested in at the moment. I couldn't take my eyes off the raven-haired creature dancing ever so seductively.

On her hands were a pair of white gloves, her feet wore white high heels that shimmered like her stones. No, she wasn't completely naked. She had a pair of gloves, shoes and hundreds of diamonds on, that was just enough.

Her belly began to sway like a belly dancer. *Eyes don't fail me now.* I was loving every move that bottom made. She was perfect, slim but not so thin that I couldn't relish every curve that made her a feminine woman.

I took a deep breath, trying to calm my pounding heart. She must have heard it. She stopped thrusting her hips mid-way through a drumbeat. Slowly, her head turned my way and I saw her face. In the center of her forehead was a diamond which matched several surrounding her navel. Instead of tiny hairs like a happy trail, this woman had diamonds.

"I knew you'd come," she said. "Did you bring back my secrets?"

My hand raised and I saw that in it was indeed the diary notebook. Where did this come from? I tried to remember where Martin had put it. Shockingly, I placed the book down on the table.

Her gloved hand touched my chin, and I gazed up at the most innocent silver-blue colored eyes. Not being able to stop myself, I moved in and kissed her. Her arms wrapped around me, and I folded to her like glue. At this point, I didn't care if she was deadly or not. I didn't give a damn that there was more money in the stones surrounding me than I could ever make in a lifetime. It was all about this woman.

Danger, now that is what draws a man. Martin was right, I realized. If he could have a woman with flaming red hair then why couldn't I kiss this deadly woman just once more? Sure her mind might not be totally normal, lusting after gems so, but neither am I. I couldn't stop watching baseball if I tried. Maybe we're alike that way, me and baseball, her and diamonds.

What's the difference? Of course, I'd never stolen anything to get a good seat in the stadium.

As I chuckled, her fingers moved and removed my shirt in one big swoop. She didn't stop kissing me. Her lips moved over my chin and down around my neck where she blew ever so softly into my ear.

Now my mind couldn't focus even if I was at the greatest Cubs baseball game ever, even if I'd wanted to.

I unfastened my pants and pushed her back down onto the table. What happened next felt even more like a dream. I'd never imagined making love could feel like this. The whole world seemed to go away except for our bodies clinging to each other with so much passion I didn't dare stop.

Our bodies molded together, and my manhood met her every thrust. She moved beneath me like a champion. Her belly rolled and made circles making me want her so badly I didn't dare take my eyes off of her.

It didn't take me long to notice her enjoying what was happening. Her eyes rolled up as she quivered beneath me and I claimed her as my mate by giving her my seed. Slowly I pulled away, realizing that my private part no longer hurt at all. Somehow, it felt more alive than ever.

Her mouth said these words, "Now you've done it."

She rose slightly and lowered her hand to the side of the table. In a flash I saw the knife clutched in her fingers. It was huge with a black widow spider on the handle. Its twisted blade shimmered as it came down straight for my heart.

I screamed.

As I was falling out of bed, my head hit the floor. Ouch, that hurt. I stared at the dust bunnies under the mattress and quickly came to know the truth. My making love to Blackie Widow had been just a dream. The Diamond Princess was nowhere near me and there was no hole anywhere on the floor. What a dream and a nightmare mixed into one! That body had felt so real in my arms, as if she had been here, making love to me.

Crawling back under the covers, I removed my shirt and put my head back down on my pillow. Across my chest I noticed a new scratch. It must have come from the car ride or the fall, I surmised. As I rolled over, I saw above the blanket something crawling toward me. It was black with a big fat belly. Eight legs were heading this way in a hurry, with fangs that were huge. It was a real black widow spider.

I sat up, grabbed my shoe and splattered the spider dead against my pillow. With the heel I turned the arachnid over, sure enough the red hourglass. My mind spun. Did she put the spider here in my apartment to scare me?

That's crazy. It must have just crawled in from the outside. I've killed these years ago even before I knew her. I knocked the dead thing off my pillow and tried to get back to sleep. The clock said three in the morning, and I had no clue as to how long I slept.

"Now you've done it," said a voice just like in my dream.

I sat up and saw Blackie standing at the foot of my bed. She leaned over and picked up the splattered spider. Suddenly, its fat belly jerked back up and came back to life. The spider crawled up her arm and hid at the edge of her sleeve. Right above the spider tattoo it stopped, almost molding to the art. Now I couldn't tell if it was a tattoo or the real spider there. Barely believing what I was seeing, I glanced back at the clock. Four o'clock. Was this just another dream?

Blackie began moving away sharply, as if mad, toward the door. Was she upset about the spider I killed? Or thought I had?

"Sorry," I said. "Those things are deadly."

"Yes, we are." she said. "Thanks for the sexual pleasures. Next time it will be your turn."

CHAPTER 8

At dawn, I went to Tye's house and knocked on the door. Martin answered already dressed in a pair of shorts and a bright blue tank top. The smile on his face told me I didn't need to ask if he had a great night with Tye.

"Good morning," I said.

"That it is," Martin replied as he began walking over to his car.

I followed him and got into the passenger's side. "She stopped by my house last night."

"Not surprised." Martin turned on the engine. "Blackie's known for that. That's why I hid her diary because I knew she'd try to get it again."

"Where is it?"

Martin gave me a look like he'd never tell me in a million years. He pulled the car onto the street and turned on the radio to a heavy metal station. Surprised it wasn't modern rap, I enjoyed the music and leaned back into the seat. After a few songs a radio announcer began telling of the history of the band and then it hit me. "What's her history?" I turned the radio knob to shut off the announcer's raspy voice.

"Don't care. All I know is the rumors and according to the IRS tax forms that she was once a nurse at a hospital."

I found that intriguing. "Don't you think if she had any problems, she would have seen a doctor at the same facility she worked at?"

A light brightened in his eyes. "I see where you're going with this."

"Don't you think we should visit the hospital and maybe check and see if there's a file on a Blackie Widow?"

Martin said, "You mean Elizabeth Blackie."

"So, she's a Beth?" She didn't look like a Beth. That name just seemed too plain for such an interesting woman. "Maybe it even lists an address."

Martin turned the car around in a flash, knocking me into the door. Glad I locked it. I watched all the pedestrians on the street scream and run out of the way of the fire-painted machine. He hit the gas pedal and the car went a few blocks and back onto the highway. I didn't ask any more questions for the length of the ride. I turned the radio back on knowing wherever I was headed might give me more clues on whom Blackie really was. I wanted to know, because rumors were nothing but lies.

Hours passed until the sun shone right above us. I was hungry. I guessed it was noon and I needed to eat something and check my blood sugar. At the next exit Martin stopped at a fast food restaurant and went through the drive through. Glad I didn't have to ask him to stop for lunch, I gave myself a quick check of the blood sugar and then engulfed the greasy burger.

Martin continued driving in a hurry, eating with one hand and chomping loudly. He raised the radio and his head bounced back and forth to the hard-core music. When he got to his last fry, he pulled onto an exit ramp and followed the blue hospital signs.

Not long after, the car pulled into the Hospital parking lot and Martin got out. "Now what we are about to do is illegal," he warned. "So, if you're out, I need to know. This is what separates the weak from us private investigators."

I exited and stood beside him. "Are you kidding? Catching criminals is what I've wanted to do my whole life."

"If you land in jail, you're on your own," Martin said. "And you don't know me."

"Agreed," I said and nodded.

"Follow me and keep your mouth shut." Martin headed toward the main entrance. He asked the old woman behind the counter where records would be because he needed to pick up an X-ray.

The elderly lady gave him directions and we followed them to the letter. In the room, there was a counter with one nurse. Behind her was a door which I could only guess led to all the hospital records.

"Ma'am, I don't want to bother you, but I seem to be in a lot of pain," Martin said, grabbing his side. "Could you please help me to the emergency room or maybe get me a doctor?"

"Oh." She came around the corner. "What seems to be the problem?"

Martin suddenly nodded to me, and I knew what to do. I rushed around the corner while the nurse's back was turned, quickly opened the door and snuck in. No one was inside. The room was full of aisle after aisle of filing cabinets. I noticed that on each row was a letter of the alphabet and I was standing right in front of A. Knowing I had to get to B, I stepped as fast as I could through the files until I saw the letter. I went to the file cabinet marked B, opened the drawer and began quickly searching through the files.

Name after name slipped past my fingers. And then I saw it, *"Elizabeth Blackie, Employee."*

I grabbed the file and rushed back to the door. I opened it slowly and saw that Martin was now practically at the door moaning in pain. Leaving the room, I leaped to stand in front of the desk then folded the file underneath my shirt to hide it.

"Oh my," Martin said. "I'm feeling better all of a sudden."

"You really should go to our emergency department. It could be your gall bladder. Would you like me to call for a wheelchair?"

"No, my friend will bring me to the front," Martin said. "Thank you, nurse." He winked, flirtatiously. "You are so cute."

The woman blushed. "Well, you go take care of yourself. Let me know if I can help you again."

Martin tossed his arm around me, pretending to lean on me for support.

We walked several yards until she went back around the desk. "You get it?" he asked.

I raised my shirt and showed him. Never had I ever done anything illegal, and the thrill was like nothing I'd ever felt before. I felt alive, like this was the very reason I was so interested in becoming an investigator in the first place.

"Let's get the hell out of here," he added.

We went back to the car and Martin pulled his hot rod slowly back onto the highway. I pulled the file out of my shirt and opened it. I began to read what it said about her, every word. It had previous addresses, a phone number and even that she had birthed one child.

A child? Was she ever married? Under the heading "Marital Status", she had written "*widow*." Interesting.

"What address does it have?" Martin questioned.

"There's two, one near the hospital and another in Florida," I said.

"Then we're off to the sunshine state." Martin changed lanes and headed south. He smiled. "The police have probably checked out all her previous addresses. But if she lived there once then chances are someone knows her. Besides I still have to look into getting us on that cruise ship."

"You mean the cruise ship with Mr. Baseball's wife who owns that giant diamond necklace?"

"You'll see," Martin said.

I flipped the page on the report and kept reading the doctor's scribbles.

"Recommend once the child is born to be put into the Florida foster care system until further evaluation. Miss Elizabeth suffers from spider delusions brought on by her own childhood abuse done by her father. She claims that the ex-boyfriend must be killed now that she is pregnant so the child can live. She claims that God put the spider tattoo on her arm to remind her that some men are evil and should not be allowed to raise their own children. The tattoo is of the black widow spider."

My heart began to pound, and I had to shut the file. So, it is an abusive past that haunts her.

"You okay?" Martin asked.

"Yeah, she's more dangerous than I thought."

"Aren't all the best women?" Martin chuckled.

I leaned back in my seat and placed my head back. Not wanting to read more, I listened to the heavy metal tunes and enjoyed the view of the brush beside the highway as we drove by.

Blackie Widow was once an abused little girl and I suddenly wanted to prove to her that not all men are evil.

CHAPTER 9

By the time we were in Florida, Martin had already read half of the file. It amazed me that anyone could read and drive at the same time. It's like half his brain was on cruise control and the other half could focus on just about anything else. He informed me that Blackie's child was still listed in foster care at a home not far from the Cape Canaveral port.

We drove for hours, the sun beating down on my skin. I couldn't stop thinking about Blackie. She had become an obsession. I wanted to learn everything about what made this woman tick. I couldn't believe how fast I fell for her and how badly I wanted just to be near her.

"You okay?" Martin asked me. "You sure haven't talked much this road trip."

"What do you want to talk about?"

"So, what did you think of my lady?" I didn't lie.

"Tye's a sweetheart."

"Nice ass, don't you think? I like 'em big and round." He licked his lips and made this smacking sound.

He might act like a player, but I figured he was hooked. "Good for you."

"You got a Juliet, Romeo?"

"Had one." The pain of the remembrance suddenly rattled through my chest. "I met her on the beach one night. I thought she was the one but she never told me how she felt about me, so I moved on."

"That's a sad story," Martin said.

"You have no idea," I admitted, not wanting to tell him anymore.

"So now you're hooked on Blackie."

"I don't want to talk about her either," I said, nodding my head to the Guns 'N Roses tune.

"No matter," he said as he pulled the hot rod off the interstate, drove about a mile and turned onto a small street.

Out of all the houses on the row, one stood out the most. It was twice as large as the others with a white picket fence, lots of kids out front and a huge swing hanging from a giant oak. The kids were screaming and playing with a tetherball. I hadn't seen one of those since I was a kid. A pole with a string and ball attached. One kid would hit it and the other would send it sailing back. What a nice way to spend a few hours.

Martin parked the car, and it quickly got the kids' attention. Many of them rushed over and gathered at the gate as we exited the uniquely flame- marked vehicle.

"Are you a pimp?" a small girl asked Martin.

"Not a professional one," he joked, as he let himself into the gate and headed towards the door.

The kids began piling over to look at the sports car. I half expected Martin to yell at them to get away, but he gave them a knowing glance to behave and kept going. That surprised me. Martin seemed to actually like kids.

He knocked on the wooden door and what answered amazed me. A woman in a two-piece suit with her blonde hair in a perfect bob cut. She had a radiant smile and perfect small features as if she could be a newswoman.

"May I help you?" she asked.

"Yeah, is this Nadia Cantina's Foster home?" Martin pulled out his wallet and showed her his private investigator's badge.

"How cool," I said, "I'm going to have to get me one of those." Her eyes widened and then changed to one of almost panic.

"I'm Nadia. Can I help you? The health department cleared my kitchen staff and the social workers come here on a regular basis," she sputtered. "We haven't had any problems at all. All of my foster children are very well taken care of."

"No, no," Martin assured her. "We're here to meet one of your kids, that's all. We're told that you have Sue Anne Blackie living here."

"Little Sue Anne," she said and smiled. "Yes, she's been with us for almost two years now."

"Can you tell us a little about her? Is she allowed supervised visits by her mother?"

"I can't give out that kind of information," Nadia replied, nervously.

I immediately wondered why she still seemed jittery. Obviously, we weren't a problem. Yet, she still shook nervously. Peering in, I noticed expensive furniture and a plasma big screen television. There were also brand-new bikes parked in a row behind the glass patio door. Interesting.

Martin was looking in too and then said, "Got quite a set up here for these kids."

"If you'll excuse me, I've just begun to have the cook make dinner."

A woman in a chef's hat just crossed the room in back of Nadia. In her hand was a pot full of potatoes. This foster home had a private chef? That seemed odd to me.

Maybe it's just my personal view, but usually foster homes aren't living this large? With this many kids, she must have had a few maids keeping it this clean. Nadia Cantina, the foster mother, must be filthy rich.

"We don't want to bother you." Martin stuck his foot in the doorway as she began to close the door between us. "We'll be on our way as soon as you point out which one is Sue Anne."

"I'm sorry. I can't give out that kind of information. Please leave or I'll call the police."

Martin pulled up his foot. The second he did, the door slammed right on us. With a turn of his shoe, Martin was in the driveway, and I followed him as he headed to the car. Then I saw her, a girl about four years old next to the bumper. Her nose had the same shape as Blackie's and her eyes were the same color.

"Are you Sue Anne?" I asked.

Her face lit up. "Are you my daddy?"

Martin couldn't believe it. Then he leaned onto the hood of the car and saw what I did: a resemblance. He didn't even question if that was her; neither did I.

"No. My name is Rome. We know your mom."

"You do?" she asked. "Where is she?"

"She don't got a mom anymore," said a young girl with wispy blonde hair.

"Her momma's dead like my daddy," a boy said.

So, Sue Anne Blackie had been lied to. "You have never met your mother Elizabeth?" I asked.

"Do you know where she is?" she shyly asked me.

I didn't, not really. I just knew the feel of her over my flesh, her nails in my back and the way those lips tasted.

"Honey, we just wanted to meet you," I said.

"My mom left me this." The girl held up a necklace. On the platinum chain was a small diamond.

For some reason a diamond that small didn't seem like something a criminal who liked giant stones would give to her only daughter. I admired it, sparkling in the sunlight, and then Martin tapped me on the shoulder.

"Let's go," he said.

"But..." Then I realized we needed to go find Blackie Widow. I don't know what made me, but I reached out and hugged the little girl very tightly. Her arms wrapped around me quickly. She broke away and said, "I like you."

"I like you too," I said and then walked away, finding it hard to do so.

The moment I opened the door, three kids piled out of the car so I could sit down. They had scuffed up the seats a bit with dirty sneakers, but Martin didn't seem to mind as he plopped down behind the wheel.

"Goodbye, pimp," said a red-headed boy.

Chuckling, he said, "My main man, leave the older ladies for me. You stay off the streets and stay in school."

"I'll do my best." He smiled.

As Martin drove away, he had to stop for a black dog with a big tan belly and matching eyebrows that was crossing the street. A stray. My eyes followed the dog to a tree where he raised his leg to pee. There I saw it written, carved into a pole, "*My Nest.*"

CHAPTER 10

A chill ran down my spine. "Did you see that?" I pointed to the pole and Martin slammed on the brakes.

His eyes told me, he understood just as I did. Nest meant spiders nest. Blackie Widow had marked her territory, which meant she had been here. That sweet little kid, Sue Anne, may not know her mother, but the mother knows she's there and keeps an eye on her.

Martin went to the end of the block, turned the car around and parked. He put back on his shades and glanced my way. "I have a feeling we'll see her if we stake out this place."

"You don't want to go back?"

"Nope." Martin took a sip off what was left in his plastic cup.

We sat there for what seemed like an eternity, watching the kids playing in the front yard. It was getting hot. I didn't realize Florida got so humid either. Wiping the sweat off my forehead, I worried about my blood sugar. I quickly took a tester out and it was 110. It was okay for now.

The sun lowered in the sky, and we sat until dark. My stomach was growling, and Martin kept squirming as if he had to piss like a racehorse. He still didn't move the hot rod even after the kids were called in by the same blonde, Nadia, who had opened the door earlier and then slammed it in our faces. One by one the lights went on upstairs in the house, and then slowly they went off.

"Maybe we should get me something to eat," I said.

"Don't you know she's here?"

"What?" I looked around the car and didn't see anything out of the ordinary. The street was empty; the place was calm as if this whole block went to bed as early as those children in the foster home.

"There she is." Martin nodded ahead.

"Where?" I spied down the street, still no one, nothing but a small Pinto which quickly passed us and turned right.

"On the roof," he said.

I glanced up and saw a shadow cross over the roof in the shape of a female body. She gripped the fire escape and pulled herself over to the window. The window was open. Checking the others, I took note that it was the only open window as if perhaps even left open for her. She crawled in.

"What now?" I asked Martin.

The light went on in the room and Martin slowly got out of the flame decorated sports car. I followed him down the street. We hid behind another parked car and watched. Blackie Widow was talking to the Nadia. They were arguing for a moment. She appeared different tonight. Her hair was tied back into a ponytail, and she was wearing a black pant suit not nearly as tight as the leather one. To me, she looked amazing in everything.

Nadia shook her finger in Blackie's face and Blackie handed her a box. Nadia opened it and smiled. Blackie headed for the door inside. Not being able to see where she was going, we kept our eyes on the blonde. Whatever was in that box sure had her attention.

A minute later Blackie quickly exited out the window. I watched how stealthily she managed to slide down the fire escape. She straightened her pant suit and went around to the back of the house.

"Let's go," Martin said, suddenly running after her.

It was hard for me to keep pace with him because he seemed to run faster than he drove. We got to the back of the house and saw her hurrying between the houses, jumping over fences, avoiding dogs and even leaping over a lawn mower. We mirrored her, doing exactly what she did until Martin fell. I glanced back only long enough to see that he had fallen over a tree branch and grabbed his ankle. Not bothering to stop, I followed her.

She ran into a bus station. I trailed her every move, bumping into people and trying to catch up. Then she ran around a corner; I did the same, only to be stopped suddenly with a quick kick to my groin.

That didn't feel good. I dropped to my knees in agony. She stood over my body as I kneeled before her.

"Leave my children alone," she said.

I wasn't about to be defeated this time by another pain in my groin. I reached out and grabbed her. As I pushed her up against the wall, my face came inches from her small nose. This close I couldn't help but gaze into those silver-blue gems again, but there was anger in them.

"Sue Anne is quite beautiful, takes after her mother," I commented. Outraged, her eyes tightened.

"Let me go." She stopped fighting me.

"Where are all the diamonds you've stolen? Where's the museum belt?" I asked. "I'll let you go, we both will if you hand over the diamonds. We especially want the diamond Egyptian belt and ring."

She smiled. "I have so many."

"Where are they?"

"Is that all you want?" she asked. Her tongue came out at me and licked my lips.

Surprised, my hands lost their strength, and she slipped out of my grasp. Instead of running away though, she simply took a step away, turned and continued staring at me with dangerous eyes.

"D-I-E-M-E-N-S," she spelled out for me. "That's all I want gone, too."

"I know about your father," I said. "He abused you and that was wrong. You can't blame all men for what one man did to you. Your boyfriend had some kind of an accident. I read the report. You can't keep this up. The cops are out for your blood now. Stones aren't worth your life. Give up. Turn yourself in."

"A mother needs to protect her children from the wicked."

Not liking riddles, I begged her, "Please, Elizabeth, I can help you."

"Spiders can escape any cage."

"You're not a spider. You're just a woman who's gone through hell." That made her very angry, the expression she gave me I'll never forget.

Rage entered her eyes, and she shoved me so hard it knocked me against the wall. I tried to grab her, but she quickly rushed off into the darkness.

Martin caught up to me, started to go after her, then saw I was standing next to a door marked *Mens*. He pushed it open, half limping. I guessed Martin must have decided that chasing Blackie on foot was pointless. Besides, it turned out he did have to pee really, really badly.

CHAPTER 11

As I was sitting at the counter of the bus station diner, Martin plopped down next to me. He grabbed the menu out of the holder and began looking it over. He didn't utter a thing for quite a while. I watched the buses coming and going through the diner window. Everyone in a hurry it seemed, with bags or briefcases in their hands.

"What can I get for you two?" a waitress chewing gum asked.

"I'll have a number three sub with extra pepperoni and jalapeños please," I replied.

"And for..." she chewed, blew a bubble and finished, "you, sir?"

"The number five sub but hold the cheese."

That was the chicken parmesan one. Maybe that would have been a better choice than the one I just ordered. Before I could tell the waitress, I'd changed my mind, she quickly trotted off to post up the order on a stick on the counter next to the cook.

"So why didn't you stop Blackie?" Martin asked.

Knowing he must be disappointed in me, I admitted, "She kicked me in my jewels."

"Well, at least we know where to find her now. Since her nest is in Florida, she won't be far away. We should probably keep an eye on that foster home and then look into when Mr. Baseball and his wife are taking their cruise."

"Do you think she'll keep going after the wife's diamond necklace?"

"The cruise ship leaves sometime in the next few weeks out of Cape Canaveral port. Every year he and his wife go to the Bahamas for their anniversary. She's a looker too and she always brings that necklace."

"The diamond necklace shaped like a black widow spider. It's almost like it was destined to be Blackie's."

"Yup, the Widow's upcoming heist according to the picture she drew in her diary. That diamond necklace is one of the most valuable on earth. Its belly piece alone is twenty carats. What makes it so unique is that inside the belly the diamond has two other diamonds inside that were natural defects in the stone. Because of their shape, like an hourglass, it looks exactly like the markings of a black widow spider. His wife being the bug scientist and all, he bought it for her. He gave it to her on their wedding night, vowing that he never wanted to live without her."

"Nice." I smiled.

"I find it sick myself," Martin muttered. Then he turned to watch the waitress filing her nails.

"You'd think she'd at least bring us our drinks."

The girl, not much more than eighteen, put down the file and began pouring our drinks. She stuffed the two plastic cups full of ice, then poured in the liquid and hurried over. Martin's cup splashed a little over the edge as she set down the drinks then she walked away.

"She's not getting a big tip," he said.

"So, you really think Blackie won't leave Florida with us hot on her trail?"

"No, she'll stay in the great Sunshine State now. There's too much here; the upcoming cruise and her kid. We might as well get a couple hotel rooms and crash after dinner. I'm beat anyway."

Thinking how much I wanted a shower, I said, "Sounds like a plan."

"You never answered me," Martin said. "Why did you let her go again?"

I nodded, having no answer. He was right. I let her run away. This was the second time now. There really was no explanation only that I really didn't want Blackie to be caught. She was haunted by an abusive past and she was just too interesting not to want to learn more. Trapped, what good was that to a spider-woman? I'd never learn more about her that way. The quest would be over and that's not what I desired most. I wanted to know everything.

When my sub came, it looked good enough. I didn't eat much of the bread and downed the meat as quickly as possible, watching Martin ignore me. He was getting good at that. His anger showed through. For a private investigator he was easier to read than my older brother at poker. Any time my brother had a good hand, his eyebrows would twist half-way to his hairline. Martin was no different. His lack of communication and smile made me know he was not too happy with what I had done.

By the time I finished Martin had been waiting a few minutes. He pulled out his wallet and paid the check. I would have, if he hadn't first. The waitress took his money and he made sure she knew, "No tip, honey. Next time bring a brother a soda, smile, and take the damn gum out of your mouth."

We left the restaurant and headed back to the car still parked in front of the foster home. Instead of moving past the house, Martin decided to climb up the gutter just like Blackie had hours ago. I watched from below as he went to the window. It was now shut, but not locked, for he quickly shoved it back open. He went inside and quickly left again the same way.

As he stood beside me I couldn't help but notice the bulge in his shirt. "Got fat all of a sudden?" I asked.

He began going to the car, so I kept pace. He split off to get behind the wheel and I jumped in to get in the passenger's side. Reaching into his shirt, he pulled out the small box that I had seen Blackie Widow hand over to Nadia.

"Open it," he ordered.

It was a small wooden box, darkly stained with no initials and a bronze clasp. I flipped open the shiny lid and inside I saw a crap load of money. I raised the first batch. There were clutches of hundred-dollar bills. I counted ten in its batch. In my lap was over one hundred thousand dollars of untraceable cash.

"Nice pay out for a day's work," Martin said and grinned. "So now we know. Blackie steals the diamonds, sells them and gives cash to the foster parent who takes care of her kid. Nadia is in on it obviously or doesn't give a damn about where the money comes from."

"You'd think Blackie would have given Sue Anne a bigger diamond," I said. "Her daughter only had a small chip."

"But her clothes were designer," Martin said. "New shoes and lots of toys, the kid probably doesn't yearn for nothing. Even that swing set and playground for all those kids looked brand new."

"All the children," I recalled. "She said, all the children. She looks at them as all her children. That's her nest. She steals to help out those kids who were abused like her or abandoned by their parents."

"Yeah, she's Robin Hood all right, except Robin wasn't a sick chick who bites and is obsessed with spiders."

I realized he had a point. Okay, maybe she wasn't innocent, but she wasn't so bad after all. I mean, there was a method to her madness. She had a good point and a bigger heart than I expected. But that blonde woman sure didn't seem too happy to be getting all that cash. Maybe it wasn't all there? Why wouldn't she have been happy about so much money?

"You should read the rest of the file tonight," Martin said, pulling the car into a fancy hotel. He parked, went to the trunk and carried a bag. He pulled out the file and handed it to me. "I think you'll learn a bit more about the Widow."

Prepared. I should have known Martin would be prepared for just such an occasion with a bag already packed with an extra set of clothes. Next time I'll have a bag. He reached in again and handed me a pair of shorts and a shirt, then zipped the bag shut.

"Thanks," I said.

Nearly twenty stories high, the hotel had massive columns in the front and large red curtains in the entrance. We walked in, checked in to two adjoining rooms, took the elevator to the top floor and went to the last two doors on the right. This was going to be a really nice hotel room. Martin planned to use some of that money so we could have a really good night's sleep.

"I'll knock in the morning," he said.

"Hey, I'm sorry about before." I was apologizing for letting the woman go.

"I don't know," Martin said.

"We're after the diamonds right, not her?" I asked.

He shoved the card key in and unlocked his door. As he opened it, he glanced my way and said, "I thought so, but what I feared is happening. You're after her heart but remember spiders don't have much of one."

CHAPTER 12

The moment I walked into the room I felt arms grab me. Large unyielding hands reached around my throat. They were pressing on both sides of my neck, and I realized I was already blacking out. Three thoughts crossed my mind as the file and clothes fell from my fingers. One, I was about to die. Two, this wasn't Blackie, and three, I couldn't see anymore.

When I woke, I found myself tied up in the back of a car. It was a big one, probably a Lincoln Town Car or an Oldsmobile of some sort. The only thing in the front seat was a driver whose hair wasn't there and whom had a neck as thick as one of my thighs. My hands were hurting me behind my back. I felt at the rope, and it was thick.

Trying to move my lips, I could see gray and realized it had been duck taped closed. Oh great. Now I couldn't move or call for help. Chances are there wasn't help anywhere to be found anyway.

I waited until the man glanced back over his shoulder. He had a big fat nose and a protruding jaw. My goodness, he was large. His eyes were bright blue like the sea and they were set deep in his head.

"You're awake." He gave me a grin.

It didn't take me long to realize why he was happy at that. He rolled the car onto a dirt path in the woods, stopped the car in front of an old, abandoned shack made entirely of wood. The door was gone but I could see movement inside and a light. I figured it must be a lantern since electricity wouldn't come this way.

The bald man climbed out of the car, opened my door and grabbed my arm, hard. He pulled me into the shack where he tossed me down to the floor. My head hit the wood. There was a smell of dust to it, and gas, lots of gas.

"So, this is Romeo?" questioned a voice. This one sounded younger.

I rolled over, shivering from more than the Florida breeze coming in. All I could see was the man from the car, but I had a better view. He was older, perhaps in his late sixties, tall and not very handsome. His teeth were slightly crooked in the front and his hairline was receding deeply in the center.

"This is the guy," replied the younger one after seeing my face.

"I'll finish it," the older man said.

The older balding man pulled out handcuffs from his back pocket and pushed me over to the wall. There he handcuffed the rope to a metal hook. I tried to pull but there wasn't any give.

"Thanks," he said. He nodded for his younger assistant to leave.

The younger man looked at me with a glimmer of sadness sparkling in his blue eyes, then left the key on the table far out of my reach and walked out of the shack. I soon heard an engine turn on and the car leave.

With a hand, the older man ripped off the tape from my mouth. I hadn't shaved since yesterday and it hurt. Although, I had the feeling this wouldn't be the last of my pain. The gas smell was almost engulfing my senses and in the corner of the room behind him I saw a can on its side, the gas still dripping to the floor, making a dripping noise every now and then.

"Who are you?" I asked.

"The real question is who are you?" said the older man.

"I'm Romeo, just like you said. I would say it's nice to meet you but that wouldn't be right." He chuckled deeply then took out a cigarette.

That wasn't good. All this gas, wooden shed, me tied up. The outcome did not look like one I wanted to picture. Where's Martin now? The big guy with all the fancy detective stuff! He can eat and drive with one hand, race faster, climb higher, but now when it comes to the actual saving my life, well, now I'm on my own.

"Got a sense of humor for a dead man," he said as he took out a small golden lighter.

"I don't know what this is about but I'm sure I can clear this up," I muttered. "I don't mean anybody any harm, especially you with the gas and the lighter."

"Sure, you don't," he said. "That's what all the bitten say." Blackie? I should have figured this was about her.

He lit his cigarette and slipped the lighter back in his pocket. He eyed me up, and then spoke around his cigarette. "I hope it doesn't get too hot in here for you."

I heard the sound of a cigarette being flicked and watched as if in slow motion as the lit end landed next to the dripping gas can. Immediately the puddle below caught fire. As the man left, he glanced back over his shoulder and gave me a smile.

I thought to myself that I would never forget a smile like that as long as I lived. Of course, seeing my situation, that wasn't going to be long anyway. That smile had this uncaring way about it, as if evil could perch on a face.

For a second I tried to run away from the wall and tried to break the hook but my hands immediately ached from the lack of ability. I tried again and again. The flames grew higher up the wall and they were coming my way very quickly.

The noises it made gave me chills down my spine. It crackled as it destroyed everything in its path, engulfing the oxygen and growing with everything it consumed.

On the table was the key. If I could only reach it! But how? Beside me was a lightweight broom so I grabbed it with my mouth, tossed it over to the table and brushed the key toward me. It knocked down to my feet.

Immediately, watching the flames build to the wooden ceiling beams, I took off my shoe and used my toes to clutch it. I tossed it up. It missed my mouth and fell back down to the floor again.

Quickly grabbing the broom with my mouth again, I hit it back over. My toes grabbed it, but the key fell out. I tried again, this time tossing the key higher. I saw it shimmering up, moved my chin forward and caught it in my mouth.

The flames were above me now, the heat was so intense, and the smoke was hurting my eyes. Trying desperately not to cough, I opened my mouth and let the key drop into my hand.

It slipped right through my index and third finger and dropped to the ground.

Without taking a second to be upset, I fought with my toe to lift the key again. Quickly, I tossed it back into the air, took it in my mouth, and dropped it down.

This time it landed in the middle of my palm. I maneuvered my fingers, grasping the lock and fighting to find the keyhole. By now, I could barely breathe. I took in a gulp of lower air and held my breath until I felt the lock click open.

"Come on!" I heard the latch fall and I leaned down just as a beam from the ceiling fell in front of me. On the floor, I crawled, following how the smoke was going. Figuring it was leaving through a door or opened window.

Not caring if I burned a bit of my pants, I crawled over the sparks falling. Barely able to see, I jumped out a doorway, out of the shack and hit the dirt and grass. My face hit a rock.

The building came crashing down like a giant bonfire. With the flames shooting to the sky, catching a tree ablaze, I marveled at how I had escaped. James Bond could not have done a better job. Maybe I was cut out for this kind of work after all. I mean if I could get out of this. Then again, don't want to do this every day, I thought, seeing the flames catching another tree branch. By now six trees were ablaze and I could hear a siren coming. Not wanting to be questioned if I had started it, I crawled to my feet and ran into the trees just as the fire truck came barreling down the road.

"Must not be that far from civilization," I said aloud as I traipsed through the bushes. After I'd walked a good hundred feet, using the moon and fire light to guide me, I found a road. I began coughing now. Must have breathed in too much smoke.

I flipped up my thumb to catch a ride, but no one stopped so I kept going. Looked like it was going to be a long walk. Just my luck. But then, luck changed. I turned the bend and saw the hotel I had just been at. Well, at least I'd get a good night's sleep after all.

CHAPTER 13

W hen I got to my floor, Martin was standing in the hallway, shutting his door. He saw me and I must have looked a mess because his expression changed to one of varied amusement. Taking a quick check down, I saw that my clothes were covered in soot and my skin was almost as dark as his.

"I knew you always wanted to be a brother," he joked.

"Thanks for wondering what happened to me," I replied.

Martin didn't ask. He handed me the black book opened to a page marked with one word, "*Mensdola*."

I recalled her license plate, "DIEMENS"'. Could that be a nickname for Mensdola, an actual person? That name looked familiar too like I had seen it before. Didn't I see that somewhere in her file? I reopened my hotel room and found the file scattered all over the floor. Quickly, I began muddling through the pages until I found the front page which I had already read. "Dr. Mensdola claims to be the father of the baby."

Reading over my shoulder, Martin gasped. "So '*Diemens*' is the father of Sue Anne and Blackie wants him dead. Now this is making sense. She thinks she's the black widow and has to kill him so her baby lives?"

"I don't buy that," I said. "I'm not so sure she's as crazy as everyone thinks. If you ask me, it's an act to scare people away. I think she's in trouble. Tonight, someone kidnapped me and almost burned me alive out in the woods. Obviously, there is some kind of blackmail going on here, maybe with the kids, too."

"You're jumping to conclusions." Martin nodded.

"This has nothing to do with my feelings for her," I pressed. "I'm telling you, Martin, if someone wanted me dead because of her then she must be in danger too."

"Or she sent him to do her deadly work," Martin disagreed, picking up the rest of the papers and muddling through them.

I sat down on my rump; my breath was a bit ragged, and I knew I should probably check my blood sugar. It had been a long, sweaty night and I really needed to get some rest. Martin on the other hand seemed quite rested and ready to begin all over again. His eyes were studying the pages as I slowly leaned back against the wall and started closing my heavy eyes.

"You okay?" he asked.

"Yeah, tired, it's not every day I almost burn to death."

"You get some sleep. I'm going to read all this and see if I can't find out some more information about the good ol' doctor." He helped me stand and walked me over to the bed. "I'll be back in the morning," was how he put it, shutting the door.

I lay down, covered myself with a blanket and before I knew it sleep came.

Only a dream could feel this good. Blackie Widow was at the foot of my bed massaging my feet, ever so slowly. She was gazing up at me with those silver-blue eyes of hers.

She only wore diamonds this time, no heels, no white shimmering gloves, just her and one giant diamond that hung between her bosoms. Now this was a dream, and you know, I was starting to really like the ones about her.

Don't know why my dreams were now filled with this one woman naked in diamonds, but for some reason it just didn't matter. Blackie Widow was the woman of my nights.

Her hands moved up under the blanket, touching my legs, her fingers twisting in my hairs. She got on all fours and began to climb up me, lifting the cover with her. I was powerless against this woman. I wanted to tell her to stop, but let's face it, I didn't really want her to.

She swayed her hips to sit on top of my pants. With her hands she ripped open my shirt and began rubbing my chest with her fingers. No one could touch me quite like her. It wasn't that she was doing anything differently from any other girl; it's just that she felt so right. I never believed much in fate, but if there is such a thing, this girl was it. She came into my museum, grabbed my diamonds and my heart all in one big heist.

"Ready?" she asked.

"Oh, yeah," I muttered.

She began kissing my neck while I wrapped my arms around her bare back. Her skin was so soft, almost like I couldn't feel her. My fingers twisted in that long soft hair which fell to her waist and all about her. My mouth went to hers, and I felt her begin.

Making love to her was easy. I didn't even need to think. It was instinctive, like something I was born to do. Watching the passion in her eyes made me never want this session to end, and oh, how quick it did.

I felt a hand shaking my body. "What?" I roared.

My eyes fluttered opened to find Martin standing beside my bed. Light had come into the room and to my horror, I realized it was already morning. He was fully dressed, had sunglasses on and had the file in his hands.

"I ordered you some eggs and toast," he said and pointed to the table.

There were two trays and coffee mugs. The smell of fresh coffee made me sit up, but I was still upset I hadn't finished that dream. Martin went over to the table and sat down. He didn't wait for me to begin. His smacking lips began to chew down a piece of toast. His eyes never returned to me; they were locked on that file.

Guessing he must have found something further, I slowly got out of bed. It was covered in soot from the fire, and I knew I had to take a bath before eating breakfast. I grabbed the extra clothes Martin gave me last night off the floor and went into the shower.

A surprise was waiting for me in the bathroom. A message on the mirror, written in blood red lipstick, the same color that Blackie Widow wore. "Martin, get in here," I said.

Martin came over with the piece of toast still in his hand. "I don't scrub backs," he said. His eyes went to the reflection. It didn't take him long to read it, "*DIEMENS AREN'T A GIRL'S BEST FRIEND.*"

CHAPTER 14

A smile rolled across Martin's face. He seemed quite amused at the discovery. "Interesting," he mumbled. "Girl likes red, red clothes and lipstick. Too bad she writes weird messages. It almost looks like blood."

Pushing Martin out, I shut the door, stepped into the shower, turned the water on and stood. Water gushed down my body and it felt good to get this grime off my body. I quickly lathered and rinsed. I hurried out and began drying off with a white towel as I stared at the message, "'*Diemens*' aren't a girl's best friend. She keeps saying, aren't…"

"Aren't a girl's best friend," that isn't how the song goes that Marilyn Monroe sang so long ago in a sexy movie. No, diamonds are supposedly a girl's best friend so why the wrong word, especially considering how many diamonds she's stolen?

I jumped into the cotton shorts and very loud shirt Martin had given me the night before. There were shades of copper and blue, all bunched up in swirls or something. The shirt actually hurt my eyes to look at, so I tried not to. Probably cost him a bundle but not my set of goods.

Opening the door, I heard a roar. It sounded almost like a plane, but it was louder coming right outside the window. Martin suddenly put down his fork, stopped chewing on an egg, and opened the curtains with one loud swoosh of the string.

My eyes must be failing me, for outside the window was a helicopter. It wasn't just any helicopter either; it was big, loud as hell, and there was a man leaning out the open side with a machine gun.

Martin's eyes widened as the first bullet broke the window. He fell under the table as I hit the floor. The bullets came so fast, I didn't have time to do anything else. I heard screaming, high pitched, coming from Martin. I glanced up only long enough to see him crawling toward me through the exploding furniture.

"Stay down!" he yelled.

He didn't need to tell me twice. On my knees and hands, we went to the door. I raised my hand to open it but the doorknob had been completely blown off. From the amount of bullet holes in it, there was barely a door left. We got out of the hotel room. In the hallway people were running for the stairs and elevators. Martin grabbed my arm and I stood. We ran fast as hell to the elevator. He hit the knob.

"We should follow the others and take the stairs," I said, just as the doors opened.

What came out at us was a familiar face. The balding man in his sixties and dressed in a Hawaiian hibiscus shirt had a gun in his hand. The younger man stood behind him, huge as ever.

"Friends of yours?" Martin asked.

"Didn't think they'd come back since they thought I was dead," I muttered, stepping into the elevator.

The ride down dragged time. The two men held guns at our backs for the first ten floors down. When we got to the third floor, Martin whirled around, kicked one man's hand and grabbed the other gun.

I'm sure he expected me to do something to help, but I just wasn't quite sure what. I saw the gun on the ground and the balding man reaching down to grab it. I kicked it out of his reach, kneed him in the stomach and gave him a punch that hurt my hand.

Martin got the gun away from the other man and that's when it happened.

Boom!

The gun went off and the bald man fell back to the floor to avoid getting shot.

The elevator door opened, and we made to leave. Martin aimed the gun back toward the elevator, waiting to see if the other man would come out. He didn't. The doors shut again, and the elevator began to rise once more.

Martin lowered the gun.

"I called the police!" screamed the man behind the lobby desk.

"Good," Martin said, leaving out the glass doors. "Tell 'em it takes a mighty black man to get the job done right."

We ran for the car, hearing the helicopter coming around the building. Martin jumped in and I did the same. The gas pedal hit the floor and we were off. I glanced back over my shoulder and saw the helicopter coming our way.

In a flash it was over us. I saw the balding man. I thought he was in the elevator. How could he be in the helicopter as well? He was making holes all over Martin's flame-painted, hot rod and Martin was not happy about it. He sped down a dirt road and headed underneath the trees.

"This should help," I said.

"This will help better." He reached underneath his seat and pulled out a rifle. It wasn't just any gun. It was long and could bring down an elephant.

In a flash he jumped into the back seat, and I took the wheel. Jumping over the emergency brake, I got in the driver's seat and kept my foot on the pedal. The trees were coming to an end, and we were about to go into a farm field.

We broke through a fence and there was the helicopter flying right over us. Martin raised the gun, aimed for the gas tank and pulled the trigger. Above us flames exploded.

Martin was knocked into the backseat as the helicopter came crashing down and just missed the back end of the car. The explosion made me deaf for a second and the flames made it hard to see. I somehow managed to pull us away to safety and over to the farmhouse.

Slamming on the brakes, I felt a hand come around the seat and a mighty tap on the shoulder.

"Not bad," Martin said.

I sighed in relief, trying to calm my heart. Martin came around and shoved me back into my side of the car. He returned the gun back under his seat and glanced over his shoulder.

"Sixteen bullet holes in my ride, now they've got me mad." Martin said. Looking over at the fireball, I guessed no survivors were possible.

There's no one to question on why Martin and I were now marked targets to be killed.

"Is being an investigator always so exciting?" I asked.

"Only if you're the bad guy." Martin grinned, starting the car.

By now, two men had run out of the farmhouse screaming in horror at what they were seeing. A helicopter news crew was headed this way, and it didn't take Martin long to keep on moving.

After all we'd been through, I had to admit this wasn't an easy ride. But I was having the time of my life. Martin didn't smile beside me; his eyes were straight ahead. He was deep in thought.

"I'm in the mood to meet the good ol' doctor," Martin said.

"Yeah," I agreed, suddenly wanting to see who had mated and survived Blackie Widow.

CHAPTER 15

The drive to the hospital proved to be a long one. We passed suburbs on long winding roads adorned with lots of palm trees. One thing about Florida, everywhere you look there's some kind of gorgeous palm tree; tall, short, bushy or with coconuts, they are always in view waving in the cool ocean breeze.

When we arrived at the hospital we were quickly turned away. *"Dr. Mensdola doesn't work here anymore"* was the response by a nurse at the front desk. She claimed he hadn't worked there for years.

"Can I see a phone book?" I asked her.

She squinted and scrunched up her nose at me. "Please," I said ever so kindly.

From under the counter, she slapped down a yellow book. Thumbing through, I found the name Dr. Mensdola, right beside the words, *Laboratory and Animal Testing Facility.'*

"Nice," Martin said, sarcastically. "We're working with Dr. Jekyll."

I jotted down the address, closed the book, gave her a quick thank you and headed back to the car. Martin drove us to the address listed. It wasn't far and there wasn't much to look at; square, large and white with a tin roof. The only words on the side were L.A.T. which I knew meant Laboratory Animal Testing. Dr. Mensdola's name wasn't to be found anywhere posted outside. We pulled in only to be quickly stopped by a guard in a booth.

"Do you have a clearance badge?" he asked, bending over next to the car. Martin showed his detective badge.

"Sorry, that's not a police badge and you don't have a warrant," the guard said.

"Now listen here, Rent-A-Cop, we've got business with Dr. Mensdola," Martin began. "We're old-time friends."

I quickly interrupted; having been store security, a guard or a rent-a-cop myself, I knew the man was just doing his job, well, I might add. "Our mistake," I said. "We'll call his house later. No problem."

Martin drove away and parked down the street. "You rent-a-guards stick together," he muttered.

"We'll just break in," I suggested. "And don't insult men making a living by protecting others ever again, Martin. Security guards bust their asses to put food on the table for their families too."

"All right." Martin leaned his head back. "Now we wait until everyone goes home for the night and then bust in."

We waited for hours until cars left in droves during a shift change. White jacketed people walked past us, waving back to the guard. They all seemed to like him. By sunset there were only a few cars left.

I tapped Martin on the shoulder. He was snoring by now. His eyes fluttered open. Without saying a word to one another that it was time, we exited the hot rod, climbed over the gate and snuck around the building. The back door was locked but there was a window left surprisingly open with a fan blowing air in for the animals in cages.

Removing the fan proved easy enough. Jumping in, Martin soon followed my lead. We were inside a room filled with trapped rabbits, rats, and cats. It sickened me to see all these animals locked up. Martin stopped by a cage with the only dog. It was huge, at least a hundred pounds, with a wagging stub of a tail. I wasn't sure what breed it was; it had a scrunched-up face

"How you doing, Big Dog?" Martin greeted, patting the dog's very large head.

The mutt licked his hand and raised his paw for Martin to shake. The lock was just silver that snapped to the right. Martin clicked it, let the dog loose and pointed to the window. It jumped out in an instant, seeking feedom.

"He knows to run the hell out of this place," Martin said. "Maybe we should let all the rest of the animals go."

Suddenly the door opened, on came the lights and a man's face dropped when he saw us. Startled for a moment, he took a step back, dropping the papers in his hand. He had dark hair, perfect model like features, and underneath his lab coat was a three-piece suit only a doctor could afford. His hand rose toward a call button.

"Dr. Mensdola?" I asked.

His hand stopped just before it pressed down to call for help. "Who are you? Do we know each other?" he asked.

"We're friends of Elizabeth's," I said, not knowing exactly what to say to him. I'd have said anything to stop him from alerting the guard in the front.

His face changed then, and a smile crossed his shaven face. I could easily see those magazine-like perfect features were the reason she fell for him.

"Elizabeth is no longer my nurse. In fact, I haven't seen that crazy girl for quite some time. They locked her up after we dated. They said she had some sort of nervous breakdown."

"Oh," I said.

"That's why we came to talk to you," Martin interrupted.

"I don't discuss my nurses with anyone," Dr. Mensdola informed, collecting his papers in one quick swoop. He sat down on a stool and began checking test tubes, lifting them up to the light. "Now if you don't mind, why don't you leave before I call the police? I have a lot of work to do."

"What exactly is your line of work?" Martin said. "You take advantage of innocent animals for what, testing make up?"

His face tightened, he put down the test tube and roared over his shoulder, "Is that what Elizabeth told you?"

"Actually, that's what I've seen with my own eyes," Martin replied.

"You have not a clue to what it takes to create. People like you sit on your high horse condemning me for performing the very test that might save your life one day with the medicines my company creates. I'm working on a cure for asthma as we speak. Thousands die from that every year. I don't mind testing animals to save humans. None of my animals die except for the insects. Don't you use bug spray around your house?" He looked me over. "Never mind, you seem to like the bugs by now."

"Did you test spiders?" I asked. "Like the black widow spider?"

"The black widow is one of the most deadly spiders in the world. We've tested many spiders to find out why people are so allergic to their neurotoxin. That's the very core with allergies and asthma. Many with these diseases produce histamines that build up in their bodies and it can even cause death. I'm trying to find the gene, the one that is defective and overreacts to grass, mold spores, things of that nature. Using such potent toxins is making that process easier and faster."

"So, you pump animals full of spider toxin?" Martin shivered. He faced us.

"Whatever I'm doing is none of your business."

"What happened to Elizabeth? Why did she go crazy? Did she try to kill you as the father of her baby?" I asked.

He raised a brow. "I told you to leave."

"We'll go as soon as you tell us more," I promised.

Dr. Mensdola reached up and pressed the button. A voice came on. "Yes, this is security."

"Call the police, Alfred, we have unexpected guests in Laboratory Twenty-three."

"Yes, Sir! I'll call and be right there."

"Thank you." Dr. Mensdola glanced back at his test tubes. "I suggest you leave before Alfred gets here. They gave him a gun last year. I'm told he knows how to shoot it."

Martin headed toward the window, but I wasn't through, not with this smug bastard who made my very skin crawl. I went to stand next to him. "I don't know what's going on or what you did to Elizabeth to make her so angry with you, but I'm going to find out."

He chuckled then. "You must have been bitten. There's anti-venom available in Lab Fourteen."

"What about your daughter, Sue Anne? She is a pretty little girl."

"Yes, she is," he said, "but I'm not the fathering kind. I'm too busy saving lives, not harming them. Now go. Your friend's even left you."

I checked over my shoulder and could hear sirens coming. Martin crashed the sports car through the fence, drove up and parked under the window. "Come on!"

"I'll be seeing you," I said to the doctor.

"Oh, I have no doubts about that," he said and grinned.

With that, I jumped out of the window onto the decorated hood. Martin gave me a nasty look, but I ignored it, climbing into the passenger's side. Two cop cars were coming with sirens blazing. Martin hit the gas pedal and we were off.

A part of me should have been worried about losing the police, but with Martin driving, I had nothing to fear. What did give me chills was that warm wet feeling breathing on the back of my neck. Glancing over my shoulder, I found our new partner who suddenly licked my nose.

"Big Dog decided to join us," Martin announced. "So that's his name now?" I asked.

"Works," Martin said as the car flew around the corner and parked in a garage. The police cars rushed past, Martin gave me a "this is too easy" glance and then we both started to smile.

Oh, yeah, did I mention I'm really starting to like this job? Finding out what happened to Elizabeth Blackie was now my main mission in life. And, I have to admit, this was much more exciting than protecting museum artifacts.

CHAPTER 16

Martin pulled his car up to an old brick house which needed major repairs to the roof. A short, built, Hispanic man opened the door, looking me up and down. Tattoos rolled down his arm. Two dragons battling on the right and on the left was a web which contained several names of women: Laura, Maria, and Stacy. "Who's the white boy?" he asked Martin.

There were two kids running around the back with diapers on. The house was a mess; even the bars on the windows were rusty and needed fixing. I peered in further and saw a girl wearing a halter top and a pair of denim shorts. She smiled at me shyly and then cradled one of the toddlers.

"He's my new partner," Martin introduced, "Name's Rome. Romeo, meet my half-cousin on my father's side, Carlos."

"Oh, a new partner now," Carlos said and nodded. "My third sister married a wop. What's he doin' on my porch, homey?"

"Question is what are you going to do for us?" Martin barged in, sat down on the sofa next to the girl and wrapped his arm around her and the kid. He flashed the young Latino angel a wink and then turned his attention back to Carlos.

"Take your arm off Anna, Marty." Carlos sneered, fixing the bandana around his head. "Don't you like 'em fatter than that?"

"Tye isn't overweight." Martin smiled. "She's big boned."

"Big bone ass, then," Carlos said and laughed then slapped him on the chest. "I don't know why you like 'em like that but to each his own. So, take your hand off my woman or I'll take it off for you."

Martin removed his arm just as Big Dog decided to jump out of the car and come inside. Big Dog suddenly knocked Carlos to the side, plodding over to Martin. He sat down beside him on the sofa. His head stood a good foot taller than Martin's. A big lick came next, wiping all the way across Martin's face.

"What the hell is that," Carlos said, "a horse?"

"It's a dog." I sighed.

"Are you sure? What do you feed that thing, Volkswagens?"

"Mexicans." Martin grinned.

"Funny." Carlos shrugged. "What do you want, cousin? Tell me what you want and then take that horse out of here before it eats one of my kids."

"I don't see the resemblance if you're cousins," I said.

Carlos pulled up a kitchen chair, plopped down in it and crossed his arms. He was completely ignoring me, and I took it as a good sign; better to be forgotten about than told to leave. I sat down on a small recliner which had massive holes in it, pushing over a few toys as I did.

"I need you to take care of Big Dog while my partner and I go on a cruise," Martin said. "It's just a four-day, three-night thing."

"Cruise, huh?" Carlos nodded. "What's my cut?"

"If everything pans out, you'll get enough."

Suddenly Big Dog started growling. His eyes tightened across the room where no one sat. My eyes focused to a giant banana spider crawling slowly up the wall. Big Dog's sounds darkened and then in one leap, he jumped across the room, bit the spider off the wall and started chomping down.

He didn't just eat the spider. His head banged it against the cement, side by side, dragging it apart. Then it gulped down the middle and licked up each leg. One dangled out his mouth, until he slurped it up.

Open mouthed, I sat shocked for a moment as Big Dog sucked down the last leg, wagged his tail then hopped back up to sit next to Martin. Martin was breathing heavy, in as much surprise as I was.

"This dog really hates spiders," Carlos said. "That's good. I've got the mall over my house."

Martin stood. "We'll be back in a few days."

"No problem." Carlos uncrossed his arms and sighed. "He doesn't kill humans like that, does he?"

"Just Mexicans." I grinned, standing.

"Your white boy's a smart ass like you," Carlos complained.

"Don't worry about Romeo," Martin said. "Take care of Big Dog and I'll be back for him. I think Tye's going to like having a guard dog around when I'm not home to protect her."

"You better come back or that thing will be on the street. I got two kids. What do I need with a dog that big? I've got enough running around my house, homey. I don't need a horse."

"See you by Tuesday." Martin turned back to Carlos' girlfriend and winked again. "See you in my dreams, sweetheart."

Carlos tripped Martin as he walked out the door. I tried not to laugh as Martin's head hit the door frame. He muttered something under his breath, trampled out the porch and back into the flame-painted vehicle.

"That dog reacted to the spider," Martin said, rubbing what was now a bump.

"He seemed trained."

"Yeah, like he was taught to do that, didn't it seem that way? I mean a normal dog will just chase a bug, maybe bark and then eat it. Big Dog attacked it, head on, no waiting, and just went for the kill."

"He might have just been hungry," I commented, thinking of my own stomach which growled.

Martin nodded. "Your stomach sounds like mine feels. Let's get something to eat, a few beers and then find a hotel. Tomorrow, we hit the port and load up for a nice trip to the Bahamas."

"Sounds good to me." I smiled.

"We're going to be working," Martin said. "So, keep your eyes on the prize, not the ladies in bikinis around the pool. That's my job. You just watch Champion, the baseball player's wife. Wherever she is that spider diamond necklace will be and that's what Blackie's going after next according to her notebook."

"Can I see if she wrote about that necklace in her diary or is it just the hand drawn picture of the diamond spider?" I asked.

"Why?"

"I just want to take a look at it," I admitted. "Maybe there's something in it you missed that might help us on the ship."

"All right, but if Blackie shows up again, don't hand it over." Martin pulled the car into the closest thing marked *"Restaurant."* It was right under the words *"Biker Bar & Shop."* He rolled the car to a stop next to several Harley Davidson motorcycles. I felt immediately out of place. You'd think Martin would too. But no, he hopped over and gave the man at the door, all eight feet, three hundred pounds of him covered in leather, a grin. "Evening," Martin greeted.

The man was not impressed. He coughed over his cigarette and muttered, "That it is."

Martin asked, "How's the food here?"

"Like crap," the man grumbled, "especially the tuna."

"Good, my Momma makes crappy tuna too." Martin waved me in.

Reluctantly, I got out of the car, looking around for any fast food joint. Any grease spot would be better than this place. As I went inside, I found Martin at a table right in the center. No one was seated around him, but they were standing all right. Martin was really out of place here, the only black man in the joint. It might as well have been the forties the way these guys were looking at him too. I walked over and sat down across the table, feeling the stares from those surrounding.

"You had to pick this place?" I asked.

A waitress came over and slopped down two beers in mugs. Her right breast was half hanging out of a tube top. I couldn't help noticing, until I saw her face. Big Dog was prettier than this woman, so I turned away.

"What can I get for ya?" she asked.

"I'll have a steak, potatoes and carrots," Martin said, looking over her very large bosom.

She grinned. "Haven't had steak since '62! Where do you think you are?"

"Then I'll have a couple hot dogs, fries and a coke please." Martin winked. "Slop on some cheese too for me, honey cakes."

The big breasted woman liked Martin. Her eyes beamed; she gave him a quick smile and then glanced down to me. "Sure thing, doll. And what will you have?"

Not wanting to wait for a menu, I said, "The same, but with onions." She scooted away and Martin watched her until she went around the bar.

His eyes shot back to me and then he pulled out Blackie's diary from underneath his shirt. "Here you go. Read 'em and weep."

"Did you learn anything from the file?"

"Yeah, I learned that she's one messed up chick that gets her rocks off on diamonds."

"Why diamonds?" I wondered, out loud. "I mean wouldn't cash be easier? Why wait for any middleman to sell to?"

"Beats the hell out of me," Martin watched the door as it reopened. "Well, what do you know?"

I glanced back, half expecting to find Carlos. I saw only someone who looked more out of place than we did: Dr. Mensdola. He was wearing a long black trench coat. With every hair in place, he walked past us and went to the bar. He ordered a shot of tequila and sat down on a stool. It didn't take me long to figure out, he didn't visit places like this dressed like that. No, he was here following us.

Why? I realized I was just about to find out.

CHAPTER 17

While the waitress brought over our hot dogs on plastic plates, the doctor glanced over, raised his shot glass and drank. He slammed the empty container down on the table, stepped off the stool and sat down beside me.

Martin raised a greasy beef dog to his mouth and began to chew. He gulped it down in a few bites and a look of utter disgust crossed the doctor's lips. By the look of him, he wasn't about to order one for himself.

"So what's up, Doc?" Martin chewed. "You actually eat here?"

"All the time," Martin said. "And you're still alive?"

"So far." Martin chuckled. "Would you like one of my hot dogs?"

"Actually, I'm here because you stole one of my dogs."

I didn't want to waste my time with small chatter. I wanted answers to several questions. Knowing Dr. Mensdola wasn't about to open up easily, I decided to play off like he was the one needing the answers. It worked in the movies. James Bond always pulled it off as if he knew everything so shouldn't it work for me? In my best confident voice I said, "We know all about what else you're doing in the laboratory."

"Did Elizabeth tell you about my own project?" he asked.

"Of course, she did," I lied.

"She did?" He seemed surprised.

"She told us all about that thingy," Martin said.

"Really?" he questioned.

"We're her friends," I added.

His eyes widened in fear and then tightened. "She wouldn't talk to either of you."

"Oh, but she informed us of all your little secrets."

"Yeah, sure she did." Dr. Mensdola raised a brow. Then came a pause as a smile crossed his lips. "At the laboratory, you mean?"

Wondering if he was on to my game already, I lied further. "Yes, at the laboratory. We know all about that."

"I bet you do," he said sarcastically. "You know everything about everything. All of it."

Martin knew what I was doing and joined in. "We know about the dog too. In fact, that's why we took him."

"So, you admit you stole my dog." Dr. Mensdola waved over the waitress. He ordered another shot and waited until she returned. He downed another drink and then ordered another. "What will it take to get the dog back to my lab?"

"Drink much?" Martin was chomping down on his second hot dog.

I began to eat as well. The taste of it was better than I expected. This was no mixed meat; this was all one hundred percent beef and it had flavor. The cheese was processed, but the onions were good.

"So how are Elizabeth and my dog?" Dr. Mensdola asked. "Are they as crazy as ever?"

"Elizabeth," Martin repeated, "told us all about you."

"Then you know about the dog?"

"Yes, we do," I lied.

"What exactly did she tell you about my dog and my project?" Dr. Mensdola pressed.

"Why don't you tell us what you think we know, and then we'll tell you if we know it." Martin smiled.

"I have a better idea. Why don't you two tell me what Elizabeth said to you and then I'll admit to you what is or isn't correct."

"No, no, you first," I said, smiling.

"So, neither of us wants to show our hands." Dr. Mensdola nodded. "Well then no dice." He slowly rose.

Martin stopped him. "Your dog is trained to kill spiders."

He sat back down. "But the main question is do you know why?"

"Of course," Martin said.

"We know all about Elizabeth, too." I said. "We know about her daughter, Sue Anne and what happened to Elizabeth when she was young."

"So, she did talk to you."

"We know about her childhood abuse." Martin sighed.

"Then you are aware that her father wore diamond rings as he took a broomstick to beat her whenever she spoke," Dr. Mensdola said.

A shiver ran up my spine. "'*Diemens*' aren't a girl's best friend."

When I said that phrase Dr. Mensdola loosened his tie and gazed into my eyes; he seemed to have heard that before. "Then you know all about her taking the diamonds and selling them for our kid and the others...there." "She gives them to Nadia. We put that much together on our own." I was right!

"So, then you know about the testing Elizabeth asked my partner to do for her? What her real obsession is?"

Martin interrupted. "Yes, we do."

"That test should have never happened. If I had known, I would have stopped it. We didn't know the effects. My partner claimed it was an accident but I'm not sure. Then all those men were bitten." Dr. Mensdola took a breath. "What have I done?"

Martin and I looked at one another, hiding our shock. We hadn't known that Elizabeth, Blackie Widow, had been a test subject. But now we did. How far had things gone? Were the effects permanent? What had Dr. Mensdola done to her? All of these questions I wanted answers to, but Dr. Mensdola rose from his chair and headed for the door.

"Wait," I ordered. He didn't, he went out the door and out into the rain.

"Damn, I left the roof down." Martin worried about his car then slapped his napkin against the table.

"Martin, did you hear him? Elizabeth had been a test subject. God knows what they did to her!"

"He might be lying," Martin said. "There's something about that doctor I don't like, Rome. He's too damn good looking for one thing. A guy with that much looks and all that money, even brains, he's going to bring a lot of trouble."

"Don't you see? Blackie really does want him dead because she was his test subject!" I gasped.

Martin started eating his fries and I began consuming what was left of mine. We didn't speak for several minutes, but I could hear his wheels turning as well as my own. Dr. Mensdola either told us a lot or was trying to get us going in the wrong direction. Either way, I had a feeling we were playing right into his hands.

CHAPTER 18

I was out by nine. Morning came and went. By noon Martin had complained about having to leave his flame-decorated hot rod behind and we were loading onto a giant cruise ship. Named, *The Sea Princess*, the mighty vessel could hold several thousand passengers with ease. We walked on board carrying a few bags. Martin was nice enough to pack one for me and I could only hope there were clothes in it that I might not be embarrassed to wear.

We walked into the ship, and I had to admit, this was quite a ship. The theme was tropical. Planted palms in pots lined the entrance, there were bamboo chairs and tables; it seemed more like an island floating at sea. There was even an aviary with two large red and blue Macaws making screeching noises above.

Passengers brushed by me, all in a hurry to get upstairs or on deck to watch the bon voyage. I glanced down at my ticket and saw I was in room 8811. Eight was my lucky number. Perhaps that was a sign that I would enjoy this journey after all. My hopes were that I could find Blackie, get her to give Martin the stolen diamonds back and ask her if she'd like me to help her. She was a woman with her whole life ahead of her. A life I hoped would somehow include me.

Blackie had been through hell as a child. After that she endured a new hell: being a test subject for Dr. Mensdola. Her quest for diamonds was because of a past abusive father who wore rings adorned with gems while he beat her with a broomstick. She sold diamonds, not for herself, but for the children at the foster home and especially for her daughter who she obviously loved enough to stay away from in the state she was in. All of this made me want to be able to show her that crime wasn't the way to protect her daughter. With rehabilitation, counseling, and a real job, perhaps she'd even be able to get her daughter back, gain custody.

Martin grabbed my shoulder and began leading me upstairs.

We're sharing a room but it's got two separate bedrooms. These tickets cost a fortune. Almost three grand for us to be traveling in style," he said. "I don't like the small rooms. They make me claustrophobic, so I got us the suite right next to who we're watching."

We passed portraits of famous actors and actresses who'd been on the ship before. I noticed how many as we went to the top deck, through a long, thin hall until we stood at door marked 8811.

As I watched Martin put in the card key, I spied a woman coming our way. Not just any woman, a blonde goddess, wearing a giant spider diamond necklace. She was thin, shapely, and on the arm of someone I knew well from watching the baseball diamond. He was so much smaller in person than he looked on television. Martin had gotten us a room right beside the baseball player and Champion, his wife.

"Wow," I muttered.

Martin glanced over his shoulder as he went into our room. "She's all that," he said, softly. "Come on."

I followed him in and saw him open a briefcase. Inside were several headsets and what looked to be a microphone. He set it up on the table, placed the microphone onto the wall, and put one of the headsets over his ears.

The room was quite spectacular. Two beds in two small rooms adjoined this one. Along the wall were giant drapes which hung open to an enormous window that looked out onto the ocean. There was a sofa, two chairs and a television set with DVD player.

"Nice," I said out loud.

"Don't get too comfortable," Martin commented, spying on the room next door with the microphone. Then he tossed down the headset. "I heard that they are planning to go for the lunch buffet after we sail off."

I went to the window and watched them untie the ship. Before long people were waving to the vessel from the dock. The ship began to turn and slowly the ship headed off into the deep, blue sea.

Martin stood beside me and smiled. "This is the life."

I returned the gesture and nodded. "So, we stake out Mr. Baseball and his Mrs. until we find Blackie Widow, right? If she doesn't come after the diamond, then we'll stake out the foster home again. Either way, we're getting some of those stolen diamonds back. Should we warn the couple?" I wondered.

"No." Martin grinned. "That's half the fun."

A knock came on our door. Martin motioned me to step out of sight while he put his hand in the briefcase. He flipped open the lining and pulled out a gun. Quickly, he pulled it behind his back. Shock washed through me as I realized he had snuck a weapon on board so easily.

"Who is it?" Martin asked.

"Don't pretend you didn't see me board. You waved!" Martin opened the door quickly and smiled. "So, I did."

The doctor entered, gave me a half-hearted smile and sat down on the sofa. He seemed nervous as he said, "I hope you don't mind my following you on the ship. You could have picked a cheaper boat!"

"You've done nothing but follow us since we left your lab," I said. "This isn't really about your dog, is it?" Martin said.

"It's about Elizabeth Blackie." Dr. Mensdola nodded, watching Martin put away his gun. "It seems the rumors are true. Those who have been bitten just can't stop loving that shrew."

"Don't call her that," I interrupted. "Why the hell are you here, Doc? Haven't you done enough damage?"

"I figured you'd lead me right to her so maybe I can talk some sense into her. She needs my help. Don't you see?"

"You come alone?" Martin asked.

"Sort of," he said.

"Sort of, is what I'm worried about."

Confused, I seated myself in the chair next to the doctor and leaned over. "Martin, is there something I don't know?"

"Should I tell him?" Dr. Mensdola asked. Martin shook his head.

"Tell me what?" I pressed, wanting to know.

"About my family." Dr. Mensdola decided to inform me regardless of Martin's suggestion. "I may be the father of Sue Anne but not the way you think. Elizabeth became pregnant by artificial insemination. She wanted desperately to have a baby. After several miscarriages, she came to my father wanting help to find out why. Modern medicine wouldn't give her the answers so since I didn't mind, we became his test subject. My father created a serum to alter her immune system while she was pregnant. Similar to allergy shots, it consisted of something far more deadly. It consisted of black widow venom. It was intended to stop her from rejecting the fetus. My father is obsessed with Blackie now. He plans to kill her and there's nothing we can do to stop him. He knows all about you two and I think he's on this ship. His car was in the parking lot."

"You knew about this, Martin?" I asked.

"Not exactly."

"So why does your father want to kill her?"

"Not just her, any person who's been bitten because the bite can trace back to him. It's in her teeth like a disease and she is the carrier. Our lab is the only one which contains black widow spiders in the state. It wouldn't take the police long to figure this out." Dr. Mensdola sighed. "I didn't want anyone to know my partner was my father. But I have to warn you, stay out of his way. He won't think twice about killing you both to get to her. The venom altered her mind and her body. My father wants to kill her, hide the body and any evidence that can connect him or our laboratory."

"What about Sue Anne?"

"My father ran test after test. Our daughter is completely normal with no traces of our serum."

"What about you?"

"My father doesn't know I was bitten," Dr. Mensdola said, raising his sleeve. On his shoulder were teeth marks. "She came to my home and bit me while I was sleeping. Ever since I've had nightmares about her, some of the dreams are wonderful, but others scare the living daylights out of me."

"Can you save Blackie?" I wanted to know.

"Yes, I believe I've created the proper antidote. I've done some tests with that dog. It's been very successful. He's healthy and seems normal enough. Even his brain patterns are absolutely normal except for the minor thing about eating spiders."

"So, it all comes out," I said.

"There's more, but I can't tell you yet." He rose. "I need that dog back. It seems you have me over a barrel now. I must have that dog. I need a little of his blood to make the serum."

Martin said. "That big dog is mine now."

"I won't harm him. I only need a vial of his blood to make more of the antidote, that's it. I only have a few more shots left. You can keep him after she's cured and no one else is bitten."

Martin winced. "One vial. We'll see."

Dr. Mensdola walked to the door and opened it. "Beware of a balding man who wears Hawaiian shirts."

I knew him well, from being tied up below him watching the walls of the shack which he had set on fire. "So that's the guy who almost burned me to a crisp. Your father!"

"You're both in a lot of danger being on this ship," he said, and with that he left, closing the door with him.

Taking a moment of reflection, I leaned back into the chair, feeling the floor gently swaying side to side. We were far out on the ocean now and there was no turning back. On board was the balding man who tried to kill us twice, the father of Dr. Mensdola. His son neither of us trusted. Martin was keeping things from me. Blackie Widow was the center of it all. The diamonds now seemed almost insignificant. Money was the last thing on my mind.

"You ready to go for lunch?" Martin asked me.

I nodded yes briefly, stood and watched Martin place the gun underneath his shirt, tucking it in under his belt. This was going to be an adventure all right. One I wasn't sure either one of us would survive.

"Do you like shrimp?" he asked.

"Not particularly," I admitted.

"Well, I'm sure they've got something you'll like," he muttered, shuffling out of the room.

Closing the door, I glanced back to my beautiful room, wishing I hadn't learned what I just had. The two Dr. Mensdolas had used Blackie Widow as a test subject all right, and I kept wondering if we weren't as well. I'd been bitten, maybe, which meant there were only two ways this was going to end. Either his father would kill me, or we would capture Blackie Widow and somehow escape.

"You think they got burgers?" I wondered.

"Have steak," Martin huffed. "I didn't pay three grand to watch you eat something you can get at one of our greasy spoons."

"Good point," I said, walking down the hall.

CHAPTER 19

And so, the plot thickens. Standing in the lunch buffet line proved to be another interesting event. Two people behind us stood the balding man who had twice tried to kill me. Behind him were Mr. Baseball and his wife, Champion. That wasn't all. I saw her. She was there.

Blackie Widow was on this ship, indeed, in this very room, heading our way.

Wearing a long red dress with a slit on one side and a long, white fur coat, Blackie Widow sashayed past me to the center of a small stage next to a white grand piano. In the center of her chest was a diamond necklace that was twice as large as the spider Champion wore. A tall, lanky man in his early twenties sat at the bench and began to play a slow, sexy melody that must have come from the early twenties.

Then I heard her voice start to sing. I was mesmerized, it was sweet and sensual. The way her mouth sang each word made me tremble right in the middle of the line. With a quick shove from Martin, I placed a ten-ounce steak on my plate, a gob of mashed potatoes and some green beans and hurried to a table right in front.

Martin sat next to me, his plate overflowing with coconut shrimp which were so large only a few dozen made such a pile. He leaned into me and said, "Watch Blackie, every move."

That wasn't going to be hard; her every move was my pleasure to observe. She swayed slightly as the song rang out. My goodness she was divine. Her hair was pulled up into a bundle of curls which cascaded down to her waist. Eyes lined black like Cleopatra and with lips as red as a rose, Blackie Widow captured my heart with each lovely note.

"Boop boop be..." Her song changed to one even Marilyn Monroe couldn't have done better. Blackie Widow knew how to get everyone to watch. She took a few steps down the platform, slowly, and strolled over to our table.

I felt her hand rub through my hair. In a brief moment between lines, she moved the microphone away from her mouth and whispered in my ear, "Hello, lover." I felt that from my toes to my brain, or what I had left of one.

She moved behind me. I turned to find Dr. Mensdola and his evil balding father. Surprisingly, the older man didn't seem to pay attention to her, but his son was. The good doctor was as smitten as I was. He grabbed her hand and kissed it gently.

Without even a second thought, the songbird moved past him and went to the baseball player's table. Her hand moved out and touched the spider diamond necklace. Champion smiled as if so many people have complimented her that this was just another moment. How wrong she was.

In Blackie's white gloved hand, the spider diamond sparkled. Her eyes twinkled with the same brilliance. That was her prize. Champion should have been a little wiser, I thought, as the diamond dropped back down around her neck.

Suddenly, Blackie Widow twirled with the music and removed her fur coat, which I hoped was faux. Now the world could see the figure beneath and it was a masterpiece. Slowly she walked back to the stage, the coat dragging behind her being held by just one finger.

The song ended.

The audience cheered and Blackie looked once behind her shoulder. "Thank you," she said. "I'll be back again tomorrow. My name's Blackie and I'll be your entertainment on this cruise. I hope you love me as much as I love to sing to each and every one of you," she bent over, her large bosom heaving over the tight bodice, "you lovers."

She walked out a door. The applause didn't end for quite a while. Without thinking of the consequences or how it would look, I rose and went after Blackie. I had to speak to her again.

When I got to the door, I saw her moving down the hall, sashaying quickly away. I ran after her as she turned a corner. When I got there, she was gone down the hall. I rushed forward at the junction, hoping to see which way she had gone.

I went down the long white hallway to the right; no one was there. To the left, it was the same thing. How could she have disappeared so fast, unless she had a room on this floor? I took a few more steps and turned back around, thinking I better tell Martin she must be staying on this level.

Suddenly, she was in front of me, standing in stilettos. I stepped back in a brief moment of shock. How did she do that? How does she disappear and reappear in a flash? Could she have stepped out of a doorway, and I missed her? Those questions would never be answered, though, because she began speaking ever so softly.

"Miss me?" she asked.

I gazed into her silver-blue eyes and smiled. "What do you think?"

"Poor Romeo. Always desiring what you shouldn't have."

"I know why you're on this ship," I informed. "You want Champion's diamond spider necklace. Could you have been any more obvious about it, Blackie?"

She tilted her head, her eyes flashed. "You really don't know me as well as you think."

"I know about Sue Anne, and that you sell those diamonds to help out all those foster kids. You were used as a guinea pig for Dr. Mensdola's father's treatments. And his son created the cure because of a very large dog. Guess I got it all down pat except where you hide the diamonds you don't sell."

"You want the diamond and stone belt, the one stolen from the museum?"

"It would be nice to return it. You did steal it on my watch. But, I don't work for the museum anymore. As you can see, I've taken on a new position."

"I like interesting positions."

"One where I help one very sick woman."

Shifting to stand on her other five-inch-high heel, she chuckled. "Who says I want a cure for what they gave me? Maybe I like how I am; no man can ever hurt me or is worth going to the grave for. I'm not to be played the fool anymore."

"I would never hurt you," I said honestly.

"Oh, but you have." Blackie Widow then held up her hand and opened it. In it was her black diary. "You stole my property, my private words and pictures. You raped my mind, lover."

"What do you mean?" I said.

It happened so fast I couldn't even take a breath to move away. Her fame came forward and bit my arm. It happened quickly and almost painlessly, but immediately I felt sick.

Hard to breathe, I felt as if it were an asthma attack. The air came out of my lungs screeching like a train. From out of her bodice came spiders, hundreds of black widows crawling down her arms onto my body.

I was covered by spiders, all of them biting me. My arms rose to smack them off of me. It didn't take long for my arms to feel too heavy to move. Around me the hall seemed to close in. Blackness overtook me. Was I was dying from poison? Blackie Widow my murderess?

CHAPTER 20

Slowly my eyes fluttered open to find Martin leaning over my body. It took my eyes a minute to focus. Breathing deeply, I glanced over my surroundings and discovered that I was back in our suite.

Had it all been another dream?

Dr. Mensdola, the younger, handsome one, suddenly grabbed my arm, examining the bite. "I think I gave him enough of the anti-venom in time."

"Think?" I asked, realizing it hadn't been a fantasy. The woman I adored had bitten me with her toxic saliva that made me pass out.

"He should be all right as long as he takes it easy for a few days," Dr. Mensdola said, walking away.

"Thanks, Doc." Martin slapped his back. "I never thought I'd be happy to see you."

"My father is the killer." Dr. Mensdola turned and faced me. "Not me. I don't like games."

"Well, thanks again." Martin led him to the door. "I'll be sure he gets rest then; we've got plenty of work to do."

Dr. Mensdola nodded and retreated. Martin returned to my bedside, plopping himself down beside me. He looked me over for a moment as if sizing me up and then gave a deep chuckle. "I told you she was deadly."

"Why do you think she bit me?"

"Why does she bite anybody? Who the hell knows what's going through any regular woman's mind let alone one who has a ton of black widow toxin in her brain." Martin scratched his short hair and tilted his head. "Are you going to be all right?"

I didn't feel that ill anymore. My head was spinning a little, but other than a slight stomachache, I was doing better. At least I wasn't going to die. To reassure him, I nodded.

A wave of relief seemed to wash over his face. Surprised he cared; I gave him a smile. Fighting the need to rest, I sat up beside him, moving my legs to hang over the side of the bed. They felt like they weighed a ton.

"When I found you in the hall you were barely breathing," Martin said. "Luckily, the young Dr. Mensdola followed me out and saw you. I wasn't even sure I could trust him but I didn't have any other choice. I didn't have the time to find another doctor. Guess he wasn't so bad after all. I mean, he gave you a shot, carried you here and then you got better within the hour."

"You think at least the son is trustworthy?" I asked him.

"Not sure," Martin admitted. "To be honest, I don't know who to trust anymore. You're bitten. Both doctors are obsessed. I may have to capture Blackie alone and get the diamonds myself."

"Why do you want all those diamonds so badly?" I wondered.

"I want the reward money," Martin began in a low tone, "to start a different life. You don't know what it's like to be so poor you have to beg the electric company, so your lights don't get shut off. My whole childhood all I remember was being worried about having no lights or having bullets coming through my house. My momma died when I was young and so I lived with my grandma in this roach-filled one room apartment. Years I went to school and got good grades to make my grandma proud. Then I went to the police academy, and I did fine. My grandma was bursting with pride until some drive-by shooter took her out when she was walking down the street to the corner market. I got him back, but it cost me my badge. I just wanted to give my grandmother a better life, you know. That 'for sale' sign was up. Just one more week, another paycheck and we would have been out of the neighborhood. My grandmother always struggled, her whole life. When I could finally give her a nice home, she was taken out, snuffed. But that's not how I'm going down. I'm going to take that reward money and I'm going to ask Tye to marry me. I'm going to buy her a house so big she can have a thousand of those stupid garden gnomes. The old thugs I grew up around will think it's a castle. Dragons couldn't even tear my new mansion down. My woman's going to have it all, everything I couldn't give my grandmother."

Feeling his pain, I nodded. "Tye's going to make you a good wife."

"She reminds me of my grandmother. I mean, well, you know, not looks wise. I mean she's good in the heart. Of course, she also has that ass that is golden too." He smiled, suddenly breaking the serious mood.

"What now?" I asked him.

"We'll just wait until the baseball hero and his wife go out again. So far all they've done since Blackie's concert is knock boots. They didn't even leave to gamble, had dessert brought up."

"Really? Get an ear full?"

"Grossed me out is more like it. That woman's louder than a Mac truck. You might as well put a horn on her."

Laughing, I suddenly forgot about being bitten.

"She got her diary notebook back, didn't she?" he asked.

"I know," I admitted, "she showed me."

"I left it in my bag when we went for dinner. So that means she knows where we are staying on board," Martin said. "From now on one of us should be awake while the other sleeps. With Blackie on board, we'll need to sleep with one eye open at all times."

"I'll take first watch," I told him.

"No, that's okay. You rest," he said, rising. He went to the small side table and pulled out a single sheet of black paper with torn edges. "She left us a page."

I took it and stared at it, my eyes focused on what was in my fingers. Across the black page was one word, actually seven letters. '*S-C-R-E-E-C- H*.' "What do you think that means?"

"I don't know, don't most people scream when they see a black widow?"

"Wait a minute," I suddenly recalled. "I saw this word before. It's tattooed on her arm right above the spider."

"What do you think it means?"

"S-C-R-E-E-C-H, it must stand for something," I said, yawning.

"Maybe it's a singer's name," he said. "Wasn't there some band in the early nineties around here with a lead singer with that nickname? Yeah, all four hot chicks playing heavy metal like the Runaways. They were bad ass!"

"But Blackie can really sing," I reminded.

"Maybe it means something like Sexy, Caring, Radical, Emotional, Evasive, and Christian Housewife?"

"Funny," I said. "No, this stands for something not made up. We'll have to figure out what." With that, I rolled back underneath the covers and put my head on the pillow. Slowly, I fell back asleep.

CHAPTER 21

By morning, we had both done a watch and Martin had overheard the couple next door discussing where to go for breakfast. We each dressed, showered, shit and shaved, then headed out the door following the couple down the hall.

Champion was laughing, quite annoyingly. She had the looks, but this donkey laugh made my skin crawl. Her famous husband didn't seem to mind though. In fact, he didn't do much but pay attention to her. As we continued turning right down a hallway, I had the feeling we were being watched.

Looking back over my shoulder, I didn't see anyone but an older gentleman walking with a cane and wearing a shirt that read, "*The Sea Princess.*" Wearing a pair of thick bubble glasses, he grinned.

I nodded a brief hello as we turned. Instead of heading straight for breakfast the couple changed their mind and went into the gambling hall. There, Martin and I sat at the quarter machines for quite some time, studying Mr. Baseball playing blackjack. He didn't take many risks for someone so rich. If his hand was over fifteen, he would never hit again. He'd rather take the loss than gamble.

The hours passed. It was nearly noon now. My blood sugar must have been getting low. Feeling a bit dizzy, I told Martin that I would be only a minute. He told me to bring him back a plate of that coconut shrimp he found so tempting the night before. In a hurry, I went to the adjoining buffet, loaded a salad and a dinner plate, which proved difficult in carrying because they were so heavy. The pot roast and chicken smelled delicious.

"Having fun?" came over my shoulder.

I turned and found the older Dr. Mensdola, carrying a plate full of pot roast which I must have missed in the line somewhere. It smelled as if it had simmered for hours. Next to the giant pieces of meat were carrots and corn in small pieces. Isn't that how it always is in a buffet, you think you've got what you want, and then you wish you would have taken something else? "Yes." I suddenly wondered if I should run instead of worrying about what was on his plate. Glancing around, I realized that Martin could no longer see me, and I'd have to handle this situation on my own.

"This will be your last vacation." He smiled with a slightly chipped front tooth.

"Perhaps yours too," I said, thinking he'll probably be arrested after I talk to the police about what he had done to me.

"My son told me that you can be trusted," he admitted, "but I don't trust anybody unless they have pure blood."

"I see," I said as I tried to step around him. He swayed to stand in my way. That's when I saw the gun, he had below the plate. I quickly concluded that yes, this was indeed the time to run. I put a fried chicken piece in my mouth, tossed the plates at him and turned to run.

Wham! The plates bounced off him and hit the floor. Everyone seated at the nearby tables stared at him covered in his own pot roast, gravy and shrimp. He gave me a look that said, "next time."

I didn't stick around to argue, I hurried out the door, back into the gambling hall. Running to Martin's side, I had forgotten about the leg hanging in my mouth.

"Is that all you got?" he complained, reaching up and grabbing it. He quickly handed it back and complained. "Can't you get anything better than fried chicken? We pay a fortune, and you get one piece of poultry! Try the shrimp, pot roast or steak or somethin'."

"I almost died," I alerted. "Daddy Mensdola was there with a gun, thank you very much. I tossed my plate at him, and he got covered in gravy and I took off."

"Do I have to do everything?" he said. "Stay here."

Before long, Martin returned with several plates full of food. He loaded mine up with pot roast, gravy, and potatoes with corn. His dish was heaping with coconut shrimp. On the side of his plate was a piece of chocolate cake.

Hungry, I began to eat but only ate half of what he'd given me so as not to raise my blood sugar too high. I concluded that Martin had been correct in picking the roast. It was much better than the chicken. In fact, this roast was so tender my fork went through the meat like butter.

"The daddy doctor wasn't in the dining hall anymore," Martin said.

"He probably needed a bath." I smiled.

Martin laughed. "Next time, just throw one of your plates so you can eat something."

"Good idea," I complimented.

For several minutes we ate. By now Mr. Baseball had lost another ten thousand in chips and his wife was yawning, tired of watching him play. He rose from the table and headed outside. They hung onto the railing for a while, watching the dolphins swim near the ship. Others were gathering as well, to watch the miracles of the sea jumping and playing in the water.

Among them came a woman in a silver bikini. Her hair was tucked under a large silver straw hat, eyes covered in big black sunglasses encrusted with diamonds. In truth, I wouldn't have known her if it wasn't for the word "Screech" and the black widow spider tattooed on her arm. She raised her glasses and smiled, looking at the dolphins.

To be honest, I'd never thought much of dolphins until now. I knew only that they were intelligent. Must be why she liked them. Blackie Widow may be many things, but stupid wasn't one of them.

I went to stand beside her, completely forgetting who I was supposed to be watching; Mr. Baseball and his wife.

"Hi," I said.

She glanced my way. "So, you're alive."

"Still," I admitted.

"Interesting," she said, walking away.

I kept pace quickly. Glancing back, Martin gave me the thumbs up, and I knew he'd keep an eye on the diamond necklace, while I continued following the potential thief.

"So, are you enjoying yourself?" she asked, returning the black sunglasses to cover her silver-blue eyes.

"Immensely." I smiled. "Except for this thing about being bitten by the most deadly spider-woman on the planet. Luckily, one of the Mensdolas gave me anti-venom to fight off your special toxin."

"I'd be happy to bite you again. All you have to do is ask, lover."

"Let's stop the small talk, sweetheart. Are you going to steal the black widow necklace or not? If so, how? And you're not going to try to kill anybody else, are you?"

"Are you game?"

"This isn't fun and games anymore, Blackie."

"Oh, don't spoil my fun." She opened a door and walked into the indoor pool room.

She removed her hat, high heeled shoes, and glasses quickly and dove into the crystal blue water near a few children playing Marco Polo. I watched her for half a second and then realized I had no other choice. Fully dressed, I jumped into the pool and grabbed her arm, pulling her up to face me.

With her wet black hair slicked back, she blinked and then kissed my cheek. Startled, I couldn't help but smile a little. The kids giggled beside us, stopping their water fun to watch.

"I'll tell you what," she said, sweetly. "I'll give you the where abouts of a few diamonds for your private investigator friend, if you leave me alone the rest of this trip, and stop asking so many questions. Chances are those doctors will take care of you both before you ever find the diamonds anyway."

"Bargaining now?"

"I web to survive. Isn't that what my kind do?"

"You're a woman, a very beautiful woman who they turned into an experiment, not a spider."

She kissed me again, this time briefly on the lips. "But I am, lover. Think about it. I'll be in 8811 tonight at nine if you want me to tell you. Meet me there."

"Okay," I said, as I watched her slowly climb the steps, her hips swaying seductively as she came out of the water. Then it hit me, I realized 8811 was my own suite.

CHAPTER 22

The rest of the day came and went. Directly at nine there was a knock. Martin went into the closet as I opened the door. She'd arrived. As she entered the room I was utterly stunned by her appearance. She wore only a white cotton robe and a pair of high heels. In her hands were two goblets and a bottle of fine champagne.

"Shall we make a toast?" She turned, her silver-blue eyes flashing.

I couldn't stop staring. Nervous, I nodded, watching her every move. She popped the cork with long red nails. Bubbles flew to the carpet, and she giggled. Wow, what a laugh. It was sweet like an angel, but she was far from that. There's a beauty to her seductiveness. I have never known such temptation before. She lacks boredom and keeps my every attention. Different than any woman I'd ever met before, she stirs my blood.

She smiled, pouring into the glasses. She took a sip off of one and handed me the other. Smelled delicious, so I took a sip. After I did, I almost choked, realizing maybe that wasn't the way to go. A cough escaped my lips.

On the bed she went, taking off her white robe. There she was, naked before me in nothing but white stiletto high heels and dark tattoos. You know I never liked tattoos on a woman before, not until now. I always thought they made a girl look like she came from the wrong side of the tracks, but not her. She could have ten more and I'd still think of her as my elegant, Spider Princess.

"Aren't you coming?" she asked.

"I think we should talk," I said, trying to remember all the things Martin wanted me to bring up; the unsold diamonds, their whereabouts, make her promise to stop, that sort of stuff that somehow didn't seem the least bit important to me as this beautiful woman was naked in my cruise ship bed.

She tilted her head and asked, "Is something wrong, lover?"

"I... don't know. You did try to kill me."

"Did I? Or did the doctors stop you from turning into something like me. Someone who would then understand the power of being like me." Suddenly, she sat up. Her eyes shined. Not the normal way a human's eyes shine, but with such a whiteness. Freaked, I jumped back. I'd never seen anything like that before. Her eyes changed as if someone had taken a picture and shined a flashlight. But there were no lights flashing here, her eyes were right in front of me, white then red.

"What are you?" I asked. "So, you weren't really trying to kill me then?"

"I am something you should have never met."

"Why me?"

"Didn't you pick me? Not I, you." She grinned. "I mean I was just there stealing a belt and you ran after me, remember?"

"Are you sorry I did?" I questioned.

"No." She slowly put on her robe again. "But you will be."

Now that her body was covered, I somehow remembered to ask, "So where are all the diamonds you didn't sell? You've stolen so many. Where are the diamond ring and the museum belt?"

"Most are forever in my web, I'm afraid. But if you must have diamonds, then you can take these." From out of her pocket, she pulled out several necklaces, bracelets and even the very Egyptian diamond and stone belt she had stolen from the museum. She laid them across the bed, displaying their beauty. Even under the one-bedroom light they sparkled; hundreds of diamonds that were worth millions.

Martin came out of the closet, uninvited. He grabbed the diamonds and began examining them. Blackie didn't even look at him because her eyes were still staring at me hauntingly.

"Thank you very kindly," he said. "This was well worth tracking you."

"You should probably leave now," she told Martin.

"What about Champion's spider necklace?" Martin asked. "You need to walk away from stealing it and certainly don't hurt anyone else. After what I've seen, spider lady, the only web you should be making is in prison."

She stood and Martin jumped back. Clearly afraid of her, he continued to back up to the wall. She didn't move towards him but me. She came to stand in front of me, peering up to me and then her eyes flashed from white back to silver. "We'll see who gets what in the end."

"Martin means you no harm," I reassured. "He cares about the reward money for the diamonds, not sending you to jail."

"Just keep the Mensdolas away from me," she ordered. "If they come near me with any... unwanted cure, I'll have to bite. Only when you become like me, can you see how much fun this really is."

"We understand," Martin said. "We have a deal then! We keep these diamonds on the bed and try to make sure both Mensdolas stay away from you with their needles while we're all on this ship."

Blackie Widow sealed the deal with a kiss to my lips. Her lips met mine ever so softly. I forgot for a moment that I'd seen her eyes changing colors, the fact she had bitten me twice, nearly caused my death, and that she was a master thief. At this second with her lips against mine, I cared nothing about those things.

She moved away, tightening up her robe. She left the wine behind as she turned toward the door.

"Don't worry," Martin said. "We'll keep the doctors away.

Blackie giggled. "Don't you know what brings a fly to the web twice?"

"No, what," Martin inquired.

"The sparkle draws it back." She went out the door.

Martin collapsed onto the bed, grabbing, clinging to the diamonds and holding them up to the light. "With the reward money for your museum belt alone we'll be rich as kings!"

"So, it's over for you?" I asked.

"Shouldn't it be?" Martin said.

"How can you say that?" I gasped. "There's a crime about to happen here. Blackie is going to steal Champion's necklace! We have to finish this, Martin. We need Blackie to be cured."

"Hey, you heard what she said. We made a deal. I don't know about you but I'm not into crossing a woman with venom. I will marry Tye and buy her a nice Florida house on the beach with this reward loot. That's all I've ever wanted. I don't give a damn about Blackie."

"Well, I do care about Elizabeth Blackie! What about Sue Anne? Doesn't she deserve her mother back?"

"That's because you're bit. It will probably go away. You'll lose that obsession over her eventually, right?"

I knew damn well I'd never forget her. The bad sure outweighed the good, but the whole time it was exciting. There was not a moment I didn't think of her. Good or bad, she owned my heart and I wanted to help her get her life back.

"You want to save her still," Martin said, softly. "The cops will capture her someday and she'll spend the rest of her life in jail!"

"Will you help me prove to the cops she's sick because of the toxin the doctors gave her?"

"No way." He shook his head, stuffed the diamond belt in his pants, and walked out the door.

I wondered if I'd ever see him again.

CHAPTER 23

The Bahamas proved to be a beautiful, magical place. As I was walking down the pier, girls with pigtails in their hair offered to brush my hair for money. Over the pale blue sea even the young were fighting for my tourist dollar.

It'd been a day since I'd seen my partner. He hadn't returned to the room and I guessed the moment the ship docked he drove out of here faster than his hot rod car ever could. Martin had what he wanted, diamonds for reward money. He obtained it legally and quite frankly would now be able to lead the life he always dreamed of.

There was just one problem; I still couldn't stop looking for Blackie. Even now, walking past the small shops selling jewelry, hats and Bahamas T-shirts, all I wanted to see was her.

The day dragged by. Alone, I went to the beach, sat by the blue water and watched the huge sun setting. I'd never felt so lonely. Here in one of the most beautiful places on earth, all I wanted was a woman I could never have. She was in my dreams, a nightmare mixed with a dream come true.

When the stars began to reflect on the water, I knew I should have stayed on the ship instead of wasting my evening shopping and sitting here. Blackie would try to steal the black widow diamond necklace if it was the last thing she ever did. I knew it and I needed a break. At least I was trying to take one out on the beach with the sand between my toes.

A couple began heading my way, there had been many before, but I knew who they were. Mr. Baseball and Champion. They looked like models walking my way near the shoreline. I never thought much of

Mr. Baseball because he always struck out against the Cubs. I glanced up at them as they passed but they paid me no mind. The sports hero laid down a towel about fifty meters away and they sat down watching the moonbeams beading across the water.

She laid her head on his shoulder. I'd never been jealous of the rich and famous before, not until now. They always seemed like non-human entities that graced the screen simply for my entertainment. These two were real people who really loved each other. I admired them and wished I had that kind of love too. It would take love like that to forget she had a laugh like a donkey.

"Miss me?" Martin plopped down on the beach beside me suddenly. Shocked, I almost gasped, but a hand shot over my mouth. He stopped me from interrupting the famous couple not far away.

"You okay, buddy?" he asked.

I nodded, and he took his hand away. Slowly, he leaned back onto his elbows and spread out his legs. In a very bright Bahamas t-shirt, he smiled while gazing down at the waves rolling in.

"Man, this is a gorgeous place," Martin said. "The drinks here are awesome! Wow!"

"Where have you been?"

"Doing my job," he said. "I've been following the couple all day."

"I thought you said you were done this case."

Martin took a deep breath and wiped some sand off of his legs. The sand was white as snow. Even in the darkness it reflected the moonlight. He shifted slightly and then raised his eyes. "Did I ever tell you the story about what happened to my first partner when I was a rookie cop?"

"No," I admitted.

"I lost him in a domestic dispute. We didn't think much of it, thought we'd just take them both into the station to take some time to calm down. I did check behind one of the living room doors and there was the guy's brother with a gun. Turned out the brother lived with them and had a bunch of coke stashed in one bedroom. The couple never expected the neighbors to call the cops. My partner was only twenty-three years old when he asked them if they minded him having a look around. The next thing I knew bullets were flying over my head and he went down. Even the couple got hit. The brother decided he wasn't going to jail for even his brother and his wife. I learned something then, don't trust anybody not even the ones you think have your back."

"I'm sorry," I said.

"I was a good cop once, before that happened. After that, I knew to put myself first," he admitted. "I am a better private investigator, though, because of all my police experience. Since I know the laws, I know how to bend things to get what I need done. Cops can't bend the law. They have to go by the book or risk losing their badge." Martin moved his legs and arms, making a beach angel in the sand.

"Did you like your partner?"

"I hardly even knew him," Martin admitted. "We'd only been together a few weeks. That's the saddest part about it, didn't know much about him. He liked lots of mustard on his hot dogs though. I remember that."

Suddenly the couple rose from their giant beach towel. Mr. Baseball brushed the sand off the back of her bikini bottom, and they started walking toward the pier.

"Looks like I'm on the move again." Martin stood. "Coming along?"

"Yeah." I rose.

"You know you remind me a lot of my old partner." Martin started to walk, and I kept pace. "He was clueless to the ways of the street. You're going to wind up getting killed if you aren't careful."

"Is that a threat?" I ask.

He pointed to the pier. The couple was far ahead now, passing a woman wearing a long red dress. She didn't move or even look their way as they went by. Blackie Widow was staring straight at us as we approached.

"Sometimes it's better not to go after a woman," he said. "It's like you're looking outside to find something real inside her. We can only imagine what it would be like for her."

"You're not making much sense, Martin." I suddenly caught my breath, realizing that in moments I would be standing in front of Blackie again.

"Just remember to duck when I say duck, okay?" he said.

As we stood in front of her, Blackie smiled. She took my arm and began to walk toward the ship. Martin stayed a few steps behind as I escorted her back to the ramp. Even though I didn't take my eyes off of her, she looked straight ahead without even saying a word.

She didn't have to.

CHAPTER 24

Parasailing. Never in a million years would I ever think that I would try it! Mr. Baseball and Champion were in front of us in line so Martin got this crazy notion that we should try parasailing too.

They hooked me up in some weird device, strapped me to a boat and the next thing I knew I was flying higher than a kite, looking down onto the most clear, pale blue water I'd ever seen.

Up here, I felt like the world was on my side. Champion was parasailing not far in front of me. Her screams, I'm sure, could be heard from the beaches below. She wasn't having as much fun as I was. Her legs were waving around in circles and her hands were gripping the cords as if she was petrified.

I hadn't seen Blackie since the night before. She gave me a wink when we entered the ship, turned left, and that was the last I'd seen of her. Martin insisted that we return to following the baseball player and his wife. In the morning light, I saw Champion was wearing the necklace even to the beach, so I knew I'd see Blackie soon enough.

Even now, floating above, Champion wore it. That necklace must have meant the world to that woman. If it got stolen, she'd probably pay a fortune to have it back. I half thought that's why Martin never walked away from the case. He knew that piece would bring him a few million more. One thing about Martin, he yearns to build Tye a big Florida mansion by the sea.

As the boat turned me around, I gazed across at all the many hotels that lined the Bahamas' white beaches. Couples and kids were in the water. At this height I could even see a marlin swimming in the middle of schools of fish.

The speed boat began to slow and gently I came down toward the beach. I remembered what they said, to run. I landed harder than expected but not badly. Martin came down beside me and patted me on the back. I glanced over to Champion. She hadn't landed so softly. Her eyes were filled with tears, and she was hugging her husband.

"I don't ever want to do that again," she cried, leaning over. "I think I hurt my lower back."

He unstrapped her, picked her up and carried her to a nearby lounge chair. "She's hurt!"

"I'll call for a medic." A steward ran off toward a hotel.

"Great," Martin said, helping me get unstrapped from the parachute. "Looks like we'll be spending our last day inside the ship's medical ward or at the hospital."

Disappointed, I nodded.

As the ambulance came, Martin and I got into a taxi and followed. Out of the corner of my eye, I noticed a car speeding up behind us. Suddenly Martin touched my arm to get my attention.

The taxi driver pulled over.

Martin said, "Keep going, driver."

Glancing behind, I saw who was behind the wheel of the car. Dr. Mensdola senior with his few grey hairs parted over his giant bald spot. A gun was in his hand, and it was coming out of the window. Suddenly, a gunshot hit the side view mirror.

The driver hit the gas pedal. We were off through the narrow Bahamas roads. The big sedan hit the taxi's bumper from behind, throwing me forward in the back seat.

"Whatever you do, don't stop," Martin ordered, pulling out his gun from his pant pocket. He leaned out the side.

Shots rang out and he flew back in. His face was sweating now, his breath was ragged as he roared, "Turn right!"

The driver did what he was told. Turning the corner, passing by small houses with fancy landscaped yards, we were struck again at the side. The driver's dreadlocks suddenly came off. He wasn't a man at all! Our driver was none other than Blackie in disguise.

A gun came around to the back seat in her right hand, pointed directly between Martin and me. She gave me a look. We both flew down just as she fired a bullet. The back window burst. The shot flew out. Lifting slightly onto an elbow, I saw that the bullet hit the windshield of the sedan, causing it to turn sideways and hit a building.

Wham!

My eyes drew to the gun. Underneath that curly, long black hair was a grin. Martin sat back up, pointing the gun at her head. "I think we'll get out of your taxi now," he said.

"Entrapped," she said and smiled.

"No more games, spider lady. Pull over and let us out," Martin demanded.

Slowly, the car came to a stop. We got out, but I wasn't done with Blackie. I wanted to know. "Why haven't you taken the necklace yet?"

"She's waiting to pounce on us and drink our insides," Martin commented, coming around to my side of the taxi. "Isn't that right, Blackie?"

"You two are over your head," she said. "You have no idea what the Mensdolas are capable of or who they would kill to cover what they've done."

"There's no need to warn us," I said. "Walk away, Blackie. The black widow necklace just isn't worth the risk. The Mensdolas won't give up on stopping you one way or another."

She glanced back. Dr. Mensdola senior was climbing out of the car and running toward the taxi. "You should have waited for me to pull over until I was a little further down the road," she said and laughed, taking off.

Martin and I looked at one another, heard another gun shot from the older Dr. Mensdola. Martin raised his gun, shot back and missed him. We started running and didn't stop for a few blocks. Quickly we raced through the shops. The father followed for a while until he started huffing and puffing and then finally quit.

"Good thing he's a lot older than us." Martin halted to catch his breath. He raised the gun for a second as if saying, "See you, later," to Dr. Mensdola Senior, and then we began walking toward the hospital.

"By now Champion's probably just being admitted anyway," Martin said.

"I say we forget about the necklace and keep watch over Dr. Mensdola. There's more to this than what we know. Sure, he'd get in a hell of a lot of trouble for that research he did on Blackie but why is he coming after us?"

"You're bitten, remember?" Martin reminded. "Now you are evidence to his crimes, too."

CHAPTER 25

We returned to the hospital only to discover Champion had been released. We then went back to our room on the ship. Martin had his listening device on the wall, hearing what was going on with intensity. Beat and tired, I took a quick shower, changed into another one of Martin's silly tourist shirts and laid down.

"Anything new?"

"Champion sprained a lower back muscle. They gave her some pain pills and now she's feeling a whole lot better. They even got busy for a while and now they are going out to eat."

"Don't they ever stop?" I commented.

"Let's go." Martin grabbed his shades and headed for the door.

We followed the couple back into the buffet line. They loaded their plates; we did as well. Martin couldn't get enough of the coconut shrimp, and me, I was too busy eating ribs.

I'd forgotten to check my blood sugar and quickly used a test strip. It was a tad bit low which meant it was time to eat.

After the couple had finished dining, they headed to a table in the back that overlooked the top deck. Their table was next to the stage. We sat beside them, trying not to be noticed.

"So, is it done?" he asked his wife.

"It is," she said and nodded. "Nadia will have the rest of the money wired."

My ears popped up. Did she just say Nadia? Wasn't that the name of the blonde foster mother at the foster home where Sue Anne lives? Martin must have heard that too because he gave me a nod and we continued to listen.

"The foster kids will be taken care of. We all win." Champion sipped on a glass of wine.

"Good, and Nadia?" he asked.

"Will lead the singer directly to Mensdola to finish cleaning our mess." Champion glanced over at us. I looked down before she could see that I was paying attention.

"Wasn't that crab good?" he asked.

"I prefer the taste of this wine. Unless it's me you'd rather have a taste of again." She smiled, changing the subject.

Suddenly, the room darkened. A spotlight hit the stage and out came Blackie Widow holding a microphone. She was wearing a dress that could only be described as barely a dress at all. Cut down to her navel, black straps covered her large breasts. The slit at her right leg was lined with red lace. Across the shoulders of the red dress was a large hooded black cape.

"Hello, lovers." She smiled, her face beaming. The crowd cheered.

"Here's a song for a celebrity in our audience. We heard he's having an anniversary so let's give a hand to Mr. Doug Anderson and his wife, Champion! He's known as the one and only Mr. Baseball."

The spotlight moved. He raised his hand, greeting the crowd, surprised. Rising to his feet, he smiled as the room burst into applause. Champion kept her composure and waved briefly as the spotlight returned to the woman on the stage.

"How about a little song I wrote just for them!" Blackie flipped her cape and did a twirl, moving closer to the couple's table.

A hip hop song began, and she sprang out a tune that would have been on the top forty in a second. "There's a man who lives his life, kissing on his beautiful wife..." She did another turn. "Love's a game that he likes to play. This bad boy has it made." The cape whirled around again as Blackie did another twist. "He's got the mansions. He's got the Benz. Now he's got my heart to bend. He's a lady killer. Oh he's fit, now it's time for him to get bit."

The teeth came out like fangs, biting him clear on the neck. It happened so fast that Champion was still smiling as her eyes widened in horror. With a quick grab, Blackie ripped off the necklace and in an instant, burst through the glass and out onto the deck.

People began screaming. Martin almost fell out of his chair, grabbing for the gun. But it was too late. Dr. Mensdola was above the baseball player's body, injecting him with a serum filled needle. Champion was on the floor, yelling to high heaven, "No! It wasn't supposed to happen this way!"

Without thinking of the sharp glass all over the floor, I ran after Blackie. I glanced back but Martin was over the baseball player's body, checking for a pulse. I kept running, following that black cape. The hood had fallen and her long black hair had cascaded down her back. She looked over her shoulder. That beautiful face with lips covered in blood.

"Stop!" I demanded. Then she jumped.

Over the railing, quicker than lightning, she leaped off the ship. She didn't fall straight down. She seemed to fly at an angle headed towards the sea. I gazed out and saw she had a line attached from the ship to a speed boat about two hundred meters away, her caped frame nearly at the edge!

She jumped down into the driver's seat of the boat, cut the line loose and started the engine. I watched her start to drive the boat away, scot-free.

I raised my hands in disgust, screaming, "Damn it!"

Blackie must have heard my scream. She smiled back at me and raised the black widow spider necklace high above her head. It sparkled, reflecting out a rainbow of different lights that shot out over the sea. It was an amazing sight, her, holding that necklace, her ultimate prize. A part of me was almost proud of her for getting what she wanted.

"This isn't over!" I yelled. "Not by a long shot. You won't get away with this! You hear me?"

She glanced back, licked her lips and returned to her seat, not to look back again.

Martin suddenly was beside me, his hand on my shoulder. He had this saddened expression on his face.

"I almost had her," I claimed.

"The baseball player barely made it," Martin announced. "She's not just a thief anymore. She nearly made a young widow out of Champion. This isn't fun and games anymore, Romeo. This Juliet is an attempted murderess."

I had to know. "Why did she sink her teeth in him so deeply? You saw the way she bit him; it was different than with me."

"Looks like we need to have a little chat with the Mensdolas." Martin grimaced. "But on our terms."

CHAPTER 26

"So how is this going down?" I asked Martin as we spied Dr. Mensdola and his son entering a room. "Should we go through the air conditioning vents and listen in?"

Martin shook his head. "This is a cruise ship, remember?"

"Oh, you mean that would be too noisy?" I wondered.

"No, too boring." Martin stepped in front of the door, pulled his gun from out of his pocket and gave a mighty kick. The door burst off its hinges and we entered, seeing the shocked expressions on the two doctors' faces.

The older Mensdola immediately reached behind his back.

Martin grimaced, shaking his own gun. "I wouldn't do that if I were you."

He sat down on the bed, keeping his hands in front of him. "I suggest you kill me because if you don't, it's only a matter of time before I succeed."

"Yeah, I heard it all before, baldy. You sure like to bark a lot, just a bunch of killing games to throw us off what's really going on with Blackie Widow."

The young doctor sat down beside his father. A hand shot through his black hair, and he took a deep breath. Nervousness made his hands tremble slightly and I knew that was the way to get my answers.

"So, how's Nadia these days?" I asked him, leaning over.

"What?" he said and gasped.

I had an idea. I had to take a shot. "You know... your real girlfriend." His eyes widened.

"There's no way... that you... could have known."

"Shut up!" The older doctor slapped his chest. "Don't you see what they are doing here? They are lying to get the answers they want. It's the oldest cop book in the trick and you are falling for it."

"Sorry, Dad. They always try to get answers from me."

"So, it's true," I gasped. "Now Blackie thinks she's the reflection of a real black widow spider which means she would only try to fatally bite the man who was the father of her child. Mr. Baseball is the real father of Sue Anne, isn't he? Champion knows and wears the spider as kind of a joke to piss her off. And let's just let me figure this out too. Blackie was starting to miscarry again, perhaps. Went to you all to help her so her body wouldn't reject this fetus and what do you do, you give her a drug that would probably kill her. Instead of killing her, it made her into something... else. She had the baby, Sue Anne was normal, so you gave the baby up to a foster home which is Dr. Mensdola's girlfriend's place. Nadia could keep an eye on Blackie that way."

The older Dr. Mensdola raised his hand to stop me. "Am I right?" I asked.

Martin slapped me on the shoulder. "You're a better investigator than I even thought. I put the girlfriend thing together, but not who the real father was. You're a bad ass."

"I know," I said and smiled. "Blackie steals diamonds not just because of her father either. Mr. Baseball owns a diamond mine in Mexico. She was trying to tell everyone that he was her target. The wife probably even helped make the drug that had done this to her. Did they even pay for the fatal injection to get rid of her?"

Martin gasped. "You the man! How the hell did you get so smart?" I shrugged my shoulders and grinned.

The older Dr. Mensdola scratched his head and asked, "So now what? You two low life's, think you're better than us because you figured out a few things. Because of Mr. Baseball we have more money than God. You two can't even dress yourselves and you think that you're going to take us down I don't even conceive of that as a possibility. We have more money, more brains, cars, houses, friends, and guns! What the hell do you have to stop us from destroying both of you and all the evidence?"

"Well, we'll just see what happens to you guys in jail," Martin said and laughed. "Funny how even the poor life will start looking good to you then."

"You have nothing on us!"

"Oh, I'd say they do." In walked a man holding out a badge.

"I'm Agent Lenny..."

The bald man reached back for his gun.

Bam!

Martin's gunshot happened so fast I barely registered what had happened. Lenny shot after Martin and struck the father straight in the center of his balding head, right where the few strands were brushed over.

"Dad!" the young doctor screamed. "You killed my father! You bastard!"

Lenny, in one big swoop, cuffed the younger doctor. "Then your father shouldn't have tried to shoot an FBI Agent."

I had never seen anyone die from being shot before and it was far worse than anything I'd seen on the movies. The breath finally escaped my lungs and came out like a screeching train. It took me a moment to realize that the faintness I was feeling wasn't from my blood sugar but from the shock.

"You okay?" Martin handed Lenny his gun. "You'll need this for evidence."

"Wow, did he know how to shoot," I said and gasped.

"You both will need to come to the ship's Security office," Lenny said. "And just for the record, Rome, I am an FBI Agent and before that I served as a Marine for ten years."

"There's nothing wrong with serving your country." Martin smiled. "Especially when you can shoot like that. Did you tape it all?"

"Sure thing." Lenny nodded. "This room is wired to the ship's security cameras."

Another man came in wearing a listening device around one ear. He was clearly wearing an FBI badge dangling on a strap around his neck. "Don't worry, Lenny. It's all on tape. I don't think you'll have a problem proving self-defense, especially with half a dozen agents as witnesses."

Martin's eyes saddened as he looked over the older Dr. Mensdola's motionless, dead body.

I didn't know what to say to Martin. He hadn't wanted this case to end with a death. I knew that it was either him or us.

Suddenly I heard what sounded like a helicopter. Peering out a port hole in the back of the room, I saw one coming.

"That chopper is for you two," Lenny announced.

"Come on, Romeo, time to go get Juliet." Martin grabbed me by the shirt and pulled me out of the room.

We didn't speak as I walked beside him to the top deck. Two ropes with harnesses lowered from the police helicopter hovering above the ship. Knowing how to fasten the latches, I quickly strapped myself in. Martin did the same with the other rope.

Martin raised a thumb up, and we were lifted into the helicopter. Tye, in what looked like a police uniform, helped lift me into the carriage.

"Tye?" My eyes questioned what I was seeing.

"Hi there, honey." She gave Martin a big kiss. "Hi, baby, miss me?"

"You know it!" Their lips locked again.

"What the hell is going on here?" I shot back.

"Did I mention I've still got a few friends on the police force and the FBI?" Martin suddenly started laughing.

The helicopter turned around and started flying west. I grabbed onto a handle as Tye maneuvered herself to sit close to Martin on the other side of the carriage.

"So, I was the fly," I realized. "For the FBI and the Police Department?"

"Yeah, and it's a good thing. Because of you we discovered the truth about all Blackie has been through. Now it's about to get real cold for the spider," Martin said.

"You're not going to hurt her, are you?" I had to know.

"Not if we don't have to." Martin shook his head. "Sorry about the lies and stuff, but we needed you."

"You mean you needed to use me," I spat out angrily, "because Blackie liked me."

"Don't feel so bad. You got the adventure of a lifetime, right? Sitting in that museum all night, every night, didn't that wear on you? Now you will return the hero who got the Egyptian diamond belt back. You might even get a raise unless you want to keep this as a new profession."

"So that's it. I was used to lure the spider into a web she can't get out of."

"To bring down the Mensdola family, yeah, he's finally getting it," Tye said and smiled. "But if it makes you feel better, we really did think you were great, in fact, great enough to help you out in case you ever want to join the police department. I just put in my transfer request to Florida. With the reward money that Martin got from those diamonds Blackie left on the bed, we will be living here soon enough!"

I realized that the last few weeks had been the best and worst of my life. "I don't know if I could be a cop."

"Come on." Martin grinned. "Don't hate the player or the uniform. No matter what the badge is you wear, it's all good versus evil, baby!"

"Blackie isn't evil," I reminded. "She's sick. She was given poison. She isn't playing with a full deck. You all want her blood all because she was protecting her daughter and the rest of the foster kids from criminals!"

"She loves being a spider lady more than she loves her daughter," Tye sighed, "or she would have taken the antidote and would no longer be the evidence the Mensdolas feared."

"So now what?" I huffed, hardly believing it. Tye partnered with the FBI and Florida PD for a major sting to trap the Mensdolas, retrieve the diamonds, and take down the most elusive thief the world had ever seen. How wrong I had been! All along they were stringing me into the web, and I didn't even see it.

"If it makes a difference, what I said about you being a bad ass, I meant that. Hell, you figured it out before us."

I leaned my head against the metal. Cold and hard, it felt just like my heart did at this moment.

"Okay, then. I know the truth and I want in," I said.

"In?" Tye questioned.

"You're going back to the foster home to arrest Nadia in the part she played in the selling of the diamonds. Now that Blackie's nearly killed Mr. Baseball, she'll go back to finish protecting her nest."

"Yes." Tye gasped. "You're right, Martin. He'd make a damn good cop!"

"Told you. Or a private investigator like me." Martin shrugged. "Heck maybe we could find him a good wife, too, one without fangs…"

"So, you're already married?" I asked them.

Tye let out the last of their secrets. "Yes, four years now."

"So, you got any kids?" I asked.

"Not yet, but we're having fun practicing." Martin winked. "Listen, I know this has got to be a hard thing for you to accept. But I do owe you a bit of gratitude for helping me bust this case, so you're in."

I should have said thank you, but at that moment, it just wasn't in me. All I could think about was what Blackie might do to Nadia now. Blackie was going to take Sue Anne away now that she had gotten her prize black widow necklace and the cops had arrested all her enemies. The cops were still after Blackie. Was I being the only thing stopping them from killing her?

Would I risk my very life to save hers? I questioned myself and immediately answered, "Yes, I'm in."

CHAPTER 27

The helicopter landed at the airport not far from Nadia Cantina's foster home. Martin's flame-decorated hot rod was waiting for us in the night. A police officer tossed him the keys, and I jumped into the back as Tye and Martin got in the front.

Martin glanced back to me as he put the key in the ignition. "This isn't going to be pretty."

"I know," I said.

"I can't make you any promises that Blackie won't get hurt. No one wants to get close enough to her to let her bite them."

"What about Champion?"

"She's being brought in for questioning along with Dr. Mensdola's son. If the doctor helps cure Blackie, he might not even see much jail time. As far as we know, the crimes were mostly done by his father and Champion. They were the ones who conducted the experiments, made the serum and injected Blackie. Blackie did the rest all by herself."

"How long has this case been going on?"

"Seven years," he admitted. "We still don't know where the diamond ring is."

As the car started and we took off like a bat out of hell, I couldn't help but feel completely betrayed. Martin had lied to me all along. He wasn't exactly who he said. Through it all, I still admired him. Funny how that is, because I learned more from him than anyone else I've ever met. He taught me how to be a private investigator. The skills would come in handy, because whatever Martin was planning, I had my own scheme.

There was some reason why Blackie gave Nadia money. At first, I thought maybe it was just her selling the diamonds to protect her daughter. There was more to it though. Now that I put together that Nadia was the younger Dr. Mensdola's girlfriend, I realized Nadia wasn't such the sweet, innocent caregiver anymore.

Martin seemed to have forgotten that. Perhaps he figures that's all there was to this story. That selling those diamonds for cash was to help out the daughter. I knew better. Blackie could and would do whatever she wanted.

She was too powerful not to. She did everything for her daughter and those kids, including allowing herself to be blackmailed.

So, the real question still lies, why did Blackie let Sue Anne stay there under the care of a woman who is tied to the *"Diemens"*, Mensdola senior, who swore to kill her. Perhaps her daughter was never in any physical danger, but it was not a good situation regardless. Why leave her at all?

There was more to this, and I was going to figure it out. Why there? Why not just take Sue Anne away herself?

"You okay?" Tye asked me. I hadn't even realized that she had been looking.

"Yes," I said.

"You still upset with us?" she questioned. "Sometimes the truth is harder to take than the lies."

"I know." I nodded.

"You're with the good guys," she reminded.

"Am I?" I wondered. "Some of the men in blue want her blood."

Martin sighed. I knew that sigh well by now. He was feeling a little guilty too for not revealing everything. We parked the car down the street. Martin waved to a man sitting on the park bench in front of the foster home. Gazing around, I saw a pattern of waves and nodding heads, one from a man fixing an electric wire dressed in uniform, another walking a dog tapped his hat. They had just signaled each other. This house was surrounded by undercover cops. If anything, we stood out the most in this ridiculous sports car with flames painted on the sides.

Just as the dawn came, the door of the home burst open and out rushed the kids. They piled up near the tree and sat on their rumps all together in rows. Nadia came out with a chair and a book. The kids cheered.

"Looks like reading hour," Martin said, putting something in his ear.

"What is that?" I asked Tye, who was doing the same.

"Here." She handed me what looked like a hearing aid.

I stuck it in my ear. There was a slight buzzing sound, but I could hear every word that was being spoken, along with every chirp of the bird above the car on a telephone wire. It sounded as loud as if the bird was twenty feet tall.

"All right, children, who knows what page we were on?" Sue Anne raised her small arm.

"Yes, Sue Anne." Nadia sat down on the chair.

 "Page twenty-three."

Nadia opened a book with a cover of a cute duck wearing tennis shoes. "Now, Sue Anne, why don't you refresh us about what we have learned so far in this story?"

"The farmer duck has a foot boo-boo," she said.

"That's right." Nadia smiled.

She was a pretty woman, Nadia Cantina. She flipped her hair back over her shoulder and caught us. She recognized us. She didn't speak for a moment; a flash of surprise washed across her face, but it quickly dissolved as she read on. "And the duck says..." Keeping the piece in my ear, I jumped out of the car.

"Where the hell do you think you're going?" Tye said. "Get your white ass back into this car."

"Thought I'd go hear about the duck with the boo-boo," I said.

"Like hell you are," Martin snipped. "Get back or you'll be in the pokey long before Nadia will be."

I didn't get to respond. Suddenly I heard a cry coming across the street. "Hi, Rome!" Sue Anne was standing, running towards the fence. "Rome! Hi!"

"Hi!" I quickly waved, smiling and hurrying across the street.

Martin rose out of his seat, huffed and sat back down. He couldn't stop me now. I was right at the gate. Sue Anne's arms waved out, calling me to come inside. The other children started to chant, "Hi! Hi!" as if happy to see me.

Nadia rose and gave a half-hearted smile. "Good morning. I see you two came back."

I reached over the gate and let myself in by unlatching the latch. When I hurried to the kids, they all embraced me. Quickly, I hugged them back. "You don't mind, do you?"

"Well, it is early for..." she stopped herself, "visitors."

"Come sit by me." Sue Anne took my hand and led me to the tree. The other children sat around me.

"You know what, kids. I've decided reading hour will be later instead. Go inside and get your coloring books, sit at your desks and I'll be right there."

The children seemed happy to oblige. They rushed off inside the house, leaving me alone with Nadia on the grass. Sue Anne glanced up at me, gave me an innocent smile, and rushed off.

Nadia slammed the book down on the chair. With rage in her eyes, she came right for me. "How dare you! I should call the police and report these visits."

"I just wanted to see Sue Anne again."

"You need to stay away. Some of these children have been through hell! I think I will call the police."

"No problem or how about the FBI." I smiled. "Which one you want?" I began pointing each agent out; the one on the telephone pole, then the dog walker.

Her eyes filled with fear. "What?"

"Sorry to rain on your parade," I said.

She quickly took my arm and started pulling me inside the house. Just as I walked up the steps, I glanced back to Martin on the hood of the car. He mouthed a few cuss words, slammed his hands down, and gave me a look that would kill.

I couldn't help but chuckle underneath my breath.

CHAPTER 28

Nadia whirled me around in the living room. I saw through the kitchen the kids were sitting around large tables. For the dozens of them, they were very well behaved. In the center of each table was a giant pack of crayons inside a Tupperware container. Books were on every seat. Each child opened their books and began coloring.

"What the hell is going on?" Nadia questioned. "What are the FBI and you two doing here? Do they know?"

"Have you heard from your boyfriend lately?" I asked her.

"Ridge Mensdola?" She gasped. "I've been worried sick!"

"Okay, I'll fill you in. Your boyfriend, the younger Mensdola doctor, is already in police custody. Mr. Baseball almost died but Ridge's father is dead..." Before I could utter another word, she was in tears. Her hands clutched her face.

"Oh, no! His father is dead! I have to go to the police station and bail Ridge out! Where is he?" she asked me. "Is he okay?"

"Sure," I said.

"Thank you for telling me!"

"I don't know where Ridge is being held," I admitted. "Last I saw him he was on the cruise ship."

"It's in port this morning," she recalled. "He's got to be at the Port Authority off of Mason Road. I've got to hurry! Please, have the FBI watch the children. I'll be as fast as I can."

She picked up her phone and dialed. "Sandy this is Nadia, something's wrong with Ridge. I have to go. It's an emergency. Will you come to the house? The FBI are here and... what's your name?" She put the phone to her chest.

"I'm Romeo," I said and grinned.

Her brows rose with the name. I was used to that. All women had this thing about my name. Lovers of Shakespeare, most girls are. "Romeo will let you in. Please get here as quickly as you can."

She rushed for the door but stopped. "Thank you," she said. "If Ridge's father is dead and Ridge is arrested, Blackie will come for Sue Anne. There's no one stopping her now."

"Do you fear Blackie?" I asked her.

"I don't have time for this." She grabbed a purse off a chair and began rushing for the door. As she opened it, Martin came in.

"What the hell do you think you're doing now?"

Nadia rushed past him, hurrying to her car. "Have the FBI stay with the children until Sandy gets here! She's a licensed Social Worker with Division of Children of Florida."

"I realize you're not an officer of the law, Rome, but even a normal person would agree that you don't warn the suspect that she's being watched by the FBI. Do you get me, there, Romeo?"

Knowing he was mad; I avoided him and went to the children. Sue Anne was coloring a picture of a caterpillar eating a leaf. She made it a bright shade of blue. The sky was yellow with a green sun. The leaf was the shade of maple brown and the stalk was blue. A smile crossed my face, as I leaned down and whispered in her ear, "Good job, Sue Anne."

Her face beamed, then she asked, "Can you stay here with me?"

"For a while," I replied, checking over artwork of the boy beside Sue Anne. He was coloring a Halloween picture of a black cat and a pumpkin. His colors were quite correct; cat black, pumpkin orange, but then again, he looked a few years older.

"Can I speak to you privately, over here?" Martin pointed to the floor next to him in the kitchen. "I can't get over how you could betray the FBI after I let you in on the truth. What's up?"

His voice was getting agitated, and the children were noticing. Some even looked his way. I decided then that it would be better for me to discuss things near the front porch than upset any of the children. I strolled over, keeping an eye on the little boys and girls who for the most part was enjoying themselves, not realizing that guns were aimed at the house from every direction outside.

"What the hell is the matter with you?" Martin lowered his voice but was making each word snap.

"You don't understand. Something isn't right here."

"Was I wrong about you, Rome? Are you turning out to be as loony as the spider lady?"

"Maybe," I admitted. "I want Blackie to know that I never meant to hurt her. This wasn't some big conspiracy on my part. I just wanted to make sure she was okay. That you all weren't going to come in here with guns blazing."

"There are kids in there," Martin reminded. "What the hell did you think we were going to do?"

"Nadia is Ridge's girlfriend, right?"

"Yeah." Martin rolled his eyes.

"Listen to me, Martin. There's a piece missing in this puzzle. I just have to find it."

Suddenly I felt a tug on my pant leg. I glanced down and saw Sue Anne holding the picture out to me. I took it, saw the funky colors and said, "Wow, you sure do like lots of colors, Sue Anne."

"For you."

"Thank you. This is adorable, just like you." I noticed the sparkle of her little diamond necklace, encircled by locks of black hair. What an amazing girl. So adorable, no wonder Blackie wanted to protect her.

"Go sit back down there, little girl," Martin said. "We're talking grown up things here with our inside voices."

"Okay," she said disappointedly, scooting away with sad eyes.

"That was uncalled for," I said, moving farther into the kitchen by the fridge. "We've got time. Blackie took a boat remember. It may take a while before she even gets near this place."

"All hell's going to break loose then," Martin reminded. "And you're standing here right in the middle. I just got word that Division of Children of Florida is sending a van to pick up these kids pronto. They won't be here when Blackie arrives."

I knew then without a doubt, they were gunning for her. Blackie had hit too many guards in the legs with stun guns, bitten too many in the past, and now she was an attempted murderess. It didn't take me long to say, "So this time are you going to be the one to shoot at her?"

Martin shook his head. "It's not like that. I am protecting the public!"

"You were bitten, weren't you? In the car, that's why you've become as obsessed as me!"

"What?" Martin gasped.

I grabbed his arm and turned it over. Just above the wrist were two puncture wounds. Through the spiffs of hair, there was no denying what I was seeing. Blackie had bitten him and he had the same toxin running through his veins as I did.

"All right, I won't deny it. Maybe that's why I've been on this damn case so long. But unlike you, I don't think she's all that. Perhaps I sucked out enough of the poison. I fear the bitch because she is dangerous. But I'm not going to break the law to kill her. All our lives are on the line here, yours and mine."

"No, her life is on the line. She was raised by an abusive father. Someone's got to stand up at the plate and make sure that she gets the chance to be helped and be a mother to that little girl in there."

"She's evil, Rome."

"She's very misunderstood."

"You're sure as hell in too deep," Martin said. "As a private investigator you have to know when to step back. You can't get personal, all right. I did with this case. I know that. But I'm not letting that ruin my total judgment. I want to take her in, alive, if at all possible."

I turned to check on the children and that's when I saw it. Above the sink was an unusual picture. It had three maple trees, similar to the one out front. In the center were several birds, cranes of some kind, long white beaks surrounding an empty picnic table.

Immediately drawn to the picture which seemed oversized for the space, I didn't even hear what else Martin was babbling on about. I walked over, reached out and pulled it off the wall. Behind it was a hole, large enough for a man to fit through and it was headed down.

Martin came up behind me. "What the hell!"

I jumped up over the sink and pulled myself into the hole in the wall. Crawling through a wooden hall, the way traveled downward into the ground. Dirt kept falling in my eyes, but I kept going, determined to find out where this led to.

"My eyes," I heard Martin complain.

He was following me in the cave, but I didn't care at this point. Where did this lead? Only a human would build an escape route large enough to fit through. It kept going down. It was so dark I couldn't see at all. My heart began to pound; I was feeling closed in and frightened. After a few more yards, it turned slightly right and there came a light in the distance.

"Wait!" Martin pulled out his cell phone to turn on what little light it gave off.

With some light, I crawled faster down until the path came to the end. It opened into a cave, a giant room about twenty-by-twenty feet. On the other side was another exit which I assumed lead out. At this point, it didn't matter. Someone had left one candle burning on a table. The same table I had seen in my dream. One candle lit up the entire cave but the corners.

Martin jumped down, closed his cell phone and gasped. "Looks like we found Blackie's nest!"

By the shine on the table, I caught view of something I couldn't believe, a web above my head. Slowly, I turned and raised my attention. Martin did the same. Together we discovered the most amazing web. Enormous, it took over the entire ceiling. The outside appeared normal, but the center was an open-heart shape filled in with large diamonds. It was almost blinding. Even though it was lit only by a candle, it was absolutely breath taking.

Martin fell to his knees, gazing up. "This is unbelievable. There must be a billion dollars' worth of diamonds made into the web."

Every space of that webbed heart was filled in with diamonds except for at the very center. Only one very small spot remained without a diamond in the web. One single, very small diamond was missing. I knew at once, Sue Anne was wearing that tiny diamond. In her own way, Blackie built this web to tell her daughter she was the center of her heart.

CHAPTER 29

My feelings of love saw the beauty of it. Even in the depths of despair, Blackie Widow created something magical, almost spellbinding. The most incredible web the world had ever seen was right on top of us.

"Let's rip this down before Blackie gets back," Martin said. "We've got millions of dollars in diamonds here."

I grabbed his shirt and looked him dead in the eye. "Like hell you're touching that web. That will bring her back. This is her nest."

Martin nodded in agreement and slowly pulled out of my grasp. "Still reeling from the bite, I see." Slowly, he pulled out a serum-filled needle. "Here, take it. When the Black Widow comes this contains the antidote. It should be enough. If not, the doctor can make more by using Big Dog's blood."

Suddenly we heard movement above. I grabbed the candle off the table and raised it above our heads. With the light above, I could see the top of the web; on it, was Champion's black widow spider necklace. It sparkled brilliantly and there was no denying what it was, or who must have just brought it.

Martin reached for his gun. With one hand he spoke into his handheld walkie-talkie. "She's in the hole... hello... this is... damn it. The walkie-talkie doesn't work down here. Man, why is it always like that for me? I think I'm doing well then wham bam, thank you ma'am I'm in danger all over with no backup."

"You got me." I waved the candle around, looking at the ceiling. Through the shadows, I saw movement crawling in the distance.

"What the hell! Is that her?" Martin roared and he ran to the hole and started screaming, "Hey, anybody up there! Hey, police, backup!"

I walked away from him, heading towards the back of the wall. Somehow, I just knew Blackie was close. It was as if I was being pulled, helplessly. She was still in control and no matter how much I denied it, I wanted her.

"Where are you going?" Martin came up behind me.

There she was, on the wall, not as I had ever seen her before. Her legs were now eight, her body an hourglass, no longer a woman, but an actual giant, black widow spider.

"Where's the bug spray when you need it?" Martin mumbled.

Unafraid, I said to her, "Blackie, I can help you." I showed her the needle.

The spider faced me, all eight giant eyes like the size of dinner plates. The fangs were as long as my arms. She raised her two front legs as if to strike.

Martin cocked his gun. "I'm not sure that's going to be enough antidote."

"No!" I yelled at him, pushing down the hand holding the gun. Suddenly, the gun fired. The spider leaped. She jumped onto the web, crawled across it and scurried out of sight. I shoved Martin hard, knocking him to the dirt. He gave me an inscrutable hard look just as a few diamonds rained down from the web.

"It's raining diamonds." Martin smiled, rising to his feet. "And I am not sticking around to be one of the '*Diemens*'."

I roared, "We're here to help, Blackie. All I've got to do is get this in you and you'll be good as new."

Martin rose to his feet, wiped himself off and raised the gun, pointing up into the blackness. "If she comes at me again, she's getting laid out. I don't care how many pretty legs she has."

I decided to try negotiations. "Blackie, please, let me help you. Wouldn't you like to get better? Wouldn't you like to be a mother to Sue Anne? She needs you. She loves you."

There was movement on the web. A few more diamonds fell, one knocking me on the shoulder. I raised the candlelight, waiting for something to spring out at me. I saw one leg's shadow move across the wall. Then one black, hairy leg came into view. She wasn't far now—far from killing me.

"She loves you, Blackie. Hell, I love you too!"

Another leg came into view. I heard Martin come up behind me. "Don't you dare," I said to him. "Give me a chance first."

"She's going to kill you!"

"If she does, she does!" I roared. "I have to try! I'm her only chance. If she bites me, then shoot her to save yourself. Now, step back!"

Martin shuffled a few paces, glancing up into the darkness. I went to the table and jumped on top. Slowly, I raised the candle to face the enormous spider's eight eyes. I'd never seen anything so frightening in my life. Yet, I knew it wasn't who she really was. It was a shield to hide her broken heart; to hide the fact that her life had been a string of bad luck. She had woven this web into something beautiful, a gift for her daughter.

"Blackie," I called, staring the creature in its frightening eyes. "Your daughter needs her mother, not this. You could give her all the diamonds in the world, and it won't be as nice as a mother's love. She needs you."

The spider raised its front legs again, showing its fangs. Drops of clear liquid, so deadly one drops the size of a pea could kill ten men, leaked out from one massive tooth.

"Sue Anne wants a mother. She's a beautiful little girl. I knew she was yours the second I saw her. All I want to do is give you what you want. It doesn't have to be like this. We can help you. With the venom you were given, no jury in the world will convict you. Not after what they did to you. You were the victim here. You didn't know what their concoction would do to you. If that wasn't enough, then when you asked for help, they denied it and took away your little girl. They blackmailed you into stealing the diamonds to make them money so they would take care of Sue Anne. Then they even tried to kill you if you didn't cooperate, to hide their crimes. We know everything,

Blackie. All you have to do is trust me. Please, just trust me and you'll be able to get your daughter back. I'll help. We might even be able to prove they knew what it would do to you, and planned this all along."

I heard Martin moving to my right. "Stay back," I roared to him.

Suddenly out of the corner of my eye I saw the web moving. The diamonds shimmering could only mean one thing, Blackie had jumped. I turned only to see the fangs rising above my head.

Bang! Rang out the shot.

Then I felt the furry mass coming down on top of me; the fangs around my neck as my head fell back and hit the table. Blackness consumed me.

CHAPTER 30

When I came to, I felt what I had in my hand: the needle. I saw that it had indeed injected the antidote right into the belly of the spider. The fangs around my neck began to move but didn't puncture my skin.

Martin was on the table, pulling the giant spider off of me. I raised her head so that the fangs didn't mark my flesh and she fell to the floor on her back, her legs curling up.

Catching my breath, I asked, "Did you shoot her?"

"I missed," he admitted. "I was shooting for her head, but she moved so quickly. You got her in the red hourglass!"

"I think it was the antidote that knocked her out," I said, plopping down on the table.

Martin crossed his legs, staring at the motionless creature. "I don't know about you, but this sure has been one hell of a long day."

Not taking my eyes off the spider, I sighed, disgusted. "I thought Dr. Mensdola said this would work. Nothing is happening."

Martin put a hand on my shoulder. "Could have been just a trick so we'd kill her off too, you know?"

"I didn't even think of that," I admitted, horrified.

"I wasn't about to let this thing take a bite out of you again," Martin said, softly. "I'm sorry that I fired my gun."

Noticing his softened tone, I saw that there was sadness in his eyes as he gazed down at the spider which was double the size of the table. He stuck the gun in the holster and said, "I'm sure she didn't really want to live like this."

"I don't know."

"I once was at this stake out where the guy used a machine gun to steal a frozen drink. No lie, he just wanted cherry, large. Didn't even think about killing the clerk, just thought hey, today's my day to get a free drink. Took out everyone in the store, he did. Now he's on death row, all for a stupid cherry drink. I changed my drink to grape after that case. After this, I am going to buy a shit load of bug spray."

My thoughts were on that little girl upstairs, now motherless. "Sue Anne. Even in this state, Blackie loved her daughter."

"As much as she could," Martin agreed. "You know, you would make a good cop. Tye was right."

"I'd make a better father," I blurted out, without thinking. Then the more I considered it, I really wanted to. Sue Anne needed a family. I may not be her biological father, but I did care about her and loved her mother. "Do you think the Department of Children of Florida would let me adopt Sue Anne on a cop's salary?"

Martin's expression changed from sadness to pleasure. A grin crossed his lips and then he said, "You like dogs? Because if you are into adopting now, I got this big thing that needs a home too. It's got a real big tongue, but don't like spiders."

"Sorry, I think he's your dog now."

He chuckled. "Well, that's okay. Guess Tye will just have to get used to the idea of that big thing roaming around."

"Big Dog will grow on her."

"Maybe I'll train him for her. He'd be the ugliest cop dog ever. What do you think?"

"I think that's great. If he takes down bad guys like spiders, he'll do just fine." I fought back my tears. If only he knew that it wasn't just the girl I had dreams of being a family to. Of all the things I've ever wanted in my life, I never thought it would be a woman with such a tragic dangerous past. Yet, she was the spice on my dish, the sparkle in my eye, the very reason I wanted to become a family in the first place. No one understood her motives more than me.

"Yeah, Big Dog will do great," Martin said. "We'll put you both in the academy."

"Is it expensive?" I questioned.

"The diamond reward money will cover just about anything you need. In fact, you don't even have to be a cop or an investigator anymore if you don't want to."

I nodded. "So, finding the web, our reward money grew?"

"Let's just say we have to share with a hell of a lot of guys, and the department house, but we'll do all right," Martin said. "Enough for me to buy that big Florida house for Tye with a big back yard for Big Dog."

"Sounds like your dreams are all coming true."

Martin nudged me. "Wish yours did too."

Suddenly at our feet was movement. We both moved away from the table and back against the wall as the massive spider rolled over and got back onto its feet. We could see bloody liquid coming from where the needle had struck the hourglass.

Martin grabbed for his gun. Again, I raised my hand in front of the chamber.

"I wouldn't do that if I were you!" Martin warned. "You might need that hand."

"Blackie!" I said. "Please, don't try to hurt us again! We are just trying to help you! The antidote didn't work, but I'm sure that we can get you another formula that will. All you have to give us is time!"

Blackie jumped onto the web, right into the center of the heart. Diamonds fell on top of us. Martin and I covered our heads with our arms, trying to block the diamonds from getting in our eyes.

"Look out!" Martin warned, just as one giant diamond hit his gun, knocking it clear out of his hands and down onto the dirt.

Then as quickly as the diamonds fell, the downpour of stones ended. We both slowly glanced up and saw the spider, ready to pounce right on top of both of us.

"This isn't good." Martin tried to move toward the gun.

Blackie made a forward movement. He stopped and so did she. "Not good at all," I agreed.

"Do something," he said, "or we're her next meal."

CHAPTER 31

Barely able to breathe from fear, I begged, "Blackie, don't hurt us."

She jumped onto the table. Her eight eyes, staring straight at us, reflected eight times. Martin reached to raise the gun, but a giant black leg kicked it from his path. He stood and backed against the wall.

"Okay, now what?" Martin gasped.

"Blackie," I tried to reason with her, "I know that you are just protecting your daughter. We don't want to hurt you, Sue Anne, or any of these kids."

The spider lifted onto its back legs; on top of the table, it towered to almost twenty feet. A giant. Our bodies moved to split apart to both sides of the cave. Martin ran left. I ran right. We did a circle around the room, hiding in the shadows behind the spider.

It turned. Martin, now only a few yards from the gun, decided to leap for it, which turned out to be a horrible mistake. Blackie jumped and struck him with her legs. His body flew and hit the back wall.

"Martin!" I yelled.

He fell to the ground, his hands rising to his head in pain. "Stop this, Blackie!" I demanded.

She turned and faced me. I wasn't about to back down and have her finish Martin off with a bite. I moved to her. She rose up as if to bite, instead of making a fast move for the gun, I smiled.

Oh, it wasn't an easy expression to get. It took everything in me to do it. I grinned like a cat that had just eaten a canary. My smile seemed to disarm her. She slowly lowered herself and began crawling up the wall.

Grabbing the gun, I ran to Martin. He was shaking his head, trying to clear his senses. "You okay?"

"I'm still alive," he mumbled. "For now," I said.

"Give me the gun." He reached for it.

I glanced up and saw the spider now on the ceiling above us. Knowing one leap would either squash us or she could sink her fangs in, I handed it to him. I didn't want anything to happen to Martin.

Martin cocked it and stood. He rose to his feet, readying to shoot at his target. There was a look in his eyes, determination. This was it. Blackie was about to die, and I knew it.

I remembered the woman who once kissed me in the hotel room. That long raven hair and that luscious amazing body. She had a confidence that made her strikingly beautiful. Underneath that giant spider, she was still that woman. Somewhere, deep underneath, she had to be.

A scream made Martin turn the gun to the hole.

Through the candlelight we could see Sue Anne looking up at her mother in terror just underneath where she must have crawled through. She cried out again, gazing up in horror at what Martin had been about to shoot. The spider jumped onto the web. Diamonds came down but this time I ignored the chance at getting hit. I knew Blackie thought Martin was going to shoot Sue Anne. She would not spare his life this time. "Drop the gun!" I roared.

Martin did what I said, just as Sue Anne's cries began to fade. The shock wore off as she gazed up at the spider. She stood there, looking up. Suddenly, the entire web shook. More diamonds began to fall, and I worried about the girl.

Why hadn't anyone been watching her? How did she know to come down here? Had she been here before?

I rushed to Sue Anne, wrapping myself over her to protect her from the falling shiny stones. When the stones stopped, I glanced up to see if I was about to be bitten. The spider hadn't moved; instead, it was changing form. The legs began sucking up into the big hourglass belly, the eyes turned inside out, and long black hair began to spill from the opening.

Martin reached down and reloaded the gun.

"Don't!" I ordered. "I think the injection is finally starting to take effect."

We stood together, us and the girl. Next the shape took that of a woman wearing nothing but a black cloth. Her hands gripped the diamonds, her two legs clutched the web and then it began to collapse, wrapping around her as she tried to stop herself from falling.

For the first time I saw fear in her those silver-blue eyes as the body and the web wrapped into one cluster, lowering to the ground. Before us stood a woman adorned in diamonds, wearing nothing but a small black cloth. From her head to her toes, she sparkled.

"That is some costume," I said to her daughter. "Maybe we could borrow it for Halloween next year?"

Martin took out his handcuffs. "You have the right to remain silent... and for damn sure the right not to bite anyone anymore."

She laughed then, kneeling to see Sue Anne. The girl gazed up at her, pointing to the enormous diamond ring on Blackie's finger.

"I've always loved you," Blackie said.

"Who are you?"

"I am the mother to all women wronged. I am your mother." The girl wrapped her arms about her neck and kissed her cheek.

"You finally came for me."

"All right," Martin said. "Enough with the reunion. Blackie, you're about to be arrested."

"Are you going to jail?" Sue Anne asked.

"Not if we get a good enough lawyer which can prove Blackie was a test subject for Mr. Baseball's wife and the Mensdola doctors," Martin told her. "But for now, your mother is going to need a lot of help and a good shrink."

I laid my hand on Sue Anne's shoulder. Blackie rose and kissed my lips, hard and fast. It took my breath away. She was no longer the spider, but she was every bit as powerful and seductive.

The kiss broke, but I knew in my heart, it would not be the last.

Hearing the cuffs go around Blackie's wrists, I smiled at her. "It's going to be all right, Elizabeth Blackie," I promised.

"Thanks," she said and grinned. "For being the mate, I didn't want to kill."

CHAPTER 32

*O**ne Year Later...***

I pulled my police car into the drive in front of a mansion overlooking the soft blue Florida seas. Instead of walking to the door, Martin and I hurried around back to a big beach party on the sand. Tables were set up under giant colorful umbrellas. Kids were playing in the water, including one who suddenly smiled back at me.

Sue Anne hurried in her pink bathing suit to my side. She jumped in my arms, and I didn't give a damn if she got my shirt damp. I gave her a quick hug and asked, "How are you, Sue Anne?"

"Mom said you two would be coming later." She gave me a hug, squishing my shiny badge with the number eight-eight-eight across it.

"Well, we got off work early," I informed.

"Hello, baby." Tye rose from underneath an umbrella, lounging on a big white chair. She gave Martin a kiss and patted him on the rump.

"Miss me?" Martin asked, knowing the answer.

"How is your case coming?" she inquired.

"Busy, not enough of these cops on the streets to round up all the thugs.

You know how it is for us private investigators," he said and chuckled. "We captured some bank robbers this morning," I said.

"Rome here climbed up the wall and pulled one down from the window. I heard all about it from a friend of mine on the force," Martin praised, slapping my back.

From out of the water came Elizabeth Blackie in a two-piece string bikini made out of white Florida sea shells. For a moment, I couldn't help but notice her every curve shimmering from the sea salt, the water pouring down her shapely legs. I didn't say another word until she came across the beach and gazed up at me with those incredible silver-blue eyes.

"Hi," she muttered. "Good day, lover?"

"Good day," I said.

"Thank goodness for that lawyer I hooked you up with," Martin said and nodded. "We wouldn't be having this beach party today."

"You think the lawyer did a good job?" I asked. "I thought he laid it on a little thick about you being her hero. We all know it really was me who saved the day."

"'*What a tangled web we weave, when first we practice deceiving.*'" Blackie turned on a barefoot heel shimmering with silver toe rings. "Thank you for the lawyer. I'm happy to just be on probation."

"You are welcome," Martin said.

I grinned, covering my eyes with a pair of sunglasses.

Suddenly Big Dog ran over a sand dune, growling at Sue Anne. With a quick jump, the dog suddenly went to bite her leg while she was in my arms. I whirled Sue Anne around so he wouldn't sink his teeth.

Sue Anne screamed, "Daddy!"

"Bad dog! Bad dog!" I roared. "Get back!"

Martin grabbed Big Dog by the collar as he growled at Sue Anne. "Sorry about that. I'll go hook him up to his chain. That was weird. I've never seen him do that before."

"Watch your dog, Martin," I ordered, lowering my girl to the sand.

Just as Sue Anne turned, smiling at the dog, her eyes shined white. "You don't want to bite me or I'll bite back." The little girl ran to her mother who was heading back to go swimming in the sea.

Oh, it isn't every spider that can swim, I thought, as I slowly crossed the sand to join them in the cool, blue ocean.

There are hundreds of thousands of orphaned, abandoned and abused children in Foster Care systems around the world. If you have a place in your home and are willing to open your heart, please consider adoption or becoming a Foster Parent. Every child deserves a safe and loving home.

Author Michele Wallace Campanelli

The Lord is near to the brokenhearted, and saves the crushed in spirit.

Psalm 34:18

ABOUT THE AUTHOR

Michele Wallace Campanelli is an American writer, singer and celebrity. During the early 1990s, Michele was lead singer of the heavy metal band, Black Widow, which was one of the first all-female bands in Florida during the early 90s. After the band, Michele Wallace Campanelli started writing short stories and fiction novels professionally. She has had nine stories appearing on the best-sellers list, including two that reached #1 on the *New York Times*. Her short stories have been included in over thirty international selling anthologies. She has also penned numerous novels, magazine and newspaper articles in both fiction and non-fiction published by Simon & Schuster, Chronicle Books, Fireside Books, Fictionwise, Florida Today Newspaper, Woman's World Magazine, Adamsmedia, McGraw-Hill, Multnomah Books, Red Rock Press, HCI and America House Publishing. Over 57 million people have read her written works internationally. In 1998, Michele wed Louis V. Campanelli III at St. Mark's UMC in Indialantic, Florida. She currently lives in Brevard with her family. When Michele isn't writing, she is CEO of Regal Entertainment Services LLC which performs concerts around Florida. She is a professional singer, writer and actor. As a devoted Christian, she uses her talents to glorify God and bring joy to others through music and her books.